I0758175

PENGUIN
PUBLISHERS

GIRL GLOW
TITAN OF TRANSFORMATION

Alexandra Elinsky, PhD

GIRL GLOW: TITAN OF TRANSFORMATION has been copyrighted in 2024.

Author Bio:

Dr. Alexandra Elinsky

2X Best Selling Author | Renown Entrepreneur | Celebrity Keynote Speaker

21X Award-Winning Author and Entrepreneur with first book, **GIRL GRIT: SAVAGE NOT AVERAGE** receiving nine literary awards within the first six months of publication:

- ➢ LitPick – 5 Star Book Award
- ➢ Infinite Generations / Positive Impact Book Awards – 5 Star Gold Book Award
- ➢ Infinite Generations / Positive Impact Book Awards – Finalist, 2025
- ➢ International Impact Book Awards – Won in 3 categories: 1) Female Empowerment 2) Feminist Advocacy and 3) Social Change
- ➢ International Impact Book Awards – Finalist, Author of the Year 2025
- ➢ BookFest 2025 – First Place Winner, Relationships and Communication
- ➢ BookFest 2025 – First Place Winner, Transformation
- ➢ BookFest 2025 – Third Place Winner, Inspiration
- ➢ Pacific Book Awards – Finalist

GIRL GRIT: SAVAGE NOT AVERAGE, is available internationally for purchase at retailers including Amazon, Barnes and Noble, Walmart, Books-A-Million and more!

Dr. Elinsky social handles –

https://www.linkedin.com/in/alexandraelinsky/

https://www.instagram.com/bossdivalibra/

*Dr. Alexandra Elinsky: (2X) #1 Best Selling Author, Celebrity Keynote Speaker, Entrepreneur, Leadership / Empowerment / Ascension Coach, Mother, and 21X Business and Literary Award Winner with 15+ years' experience coaching and training professionals globally. With clients in 20+ countries around the world, Dr. Elinsky has helped individuals achieve personal and professional excellence. Recognized time and again for business mastery and meritorious performance, she has been awarded Top International Empowerment Coach of the Decade by IAOTP, Top International Empowerment Coach of the Year by IAOTP, Empowered Woman of the Year 2025 by IAOTP, Best Coaching Services in the USA by Stellar Business, Top 5 Coaches of the Year by Female Voice Awards, 5 Star Gold Book Review (Highest Accolade) by Infinite Generations / Positive Impact Book Review, Female Empowerment, Feminist Advocacy and Social Change Book Award by International Impact Book Awards, Top 5 Most Aspiring Businesswomen by CIO Today, Global Recognition for Leadership Excellence by Global Awards, University of Akron Leadership Excellence Award, The Chicago School of Professional Psychology Distinguished Alumni Award, Empowered Woman 2024 by Empowered Magazine, 5-Star Award by LitPick Reviews, Three awards from BookFest 2025 (2 in First Place), Visionary Voice in Leadership Coaching – Human Resource, USA by Fluxx Events 2025, and Woman of the Year 2025 by the CIO Times. Gracing the front covers of business magazines CIO Today, Passionate Magazine, Conglomerate Magazine, and The Business Fame with additional recognition in ABC, NBC, and Fox news outlets, Dr. Elinsky's message of grit and transformation continues to expand globally. She was selected as part of World Magazine's 40 under 40 Emerging Leaders to Watch in 2023. Her first book, **GIRL GRIT: SAVAGE NOT AVERAGE**, was released on November 8th, 2024. Dr. Elinsky is determined to spread her message of human empowerment and self-esteem globally, spreading her fire everywhere she goes.*

Introduction

"Keep your feet on the ground and your thoughts at lofty heights" – Peace Pilgrim.

"But they that wait upon the Lord shall renew their strength; **they shall mount up with wings as eagles;** they shall run, and not be weary; and they shall walk, and not faint – Isaiah 40:31

The reason women have been in places of inferiority in society is because society has conditioned us to be inferior, which has strategically stunted our natural potential and right to empowerment as individuals and worthy human beings. Men have supported our own self-imposed limitations, leveraging their advantage by empowering themselves at our suppression because we, as women, have allowed such behavior. They acquired power as a result, and gender power dynamics formed.

You can only be powerless if you act powerless, and you can only be powerful if you act powerful. There is no other way. Power only comes from within, and so does its absence.

This is why failure is more common than success.

But it is far easier to succeed than it is to fail.

To amass power, we must be able to embody it. Only we determine who we are.

Do you worry that others are judging you? Do not worry. They are judging themselves far more critically than you.

We assume our roles in society because of predetermined structures that have existed for years. But where is it really written? Certainly not in the Bible, if you were wondering. After all, God created women and men equal because God is androgynous.

Oh, and in case no one has told you yet... men love POWERFUL WOMEN! I am LIVING PROOF!

Additional Considerations

The central theme of this book is ***power and spirituality*** leveraged to build a powerful and empowered woman. I integrate resources from different religious texts; however, this book is NOT categorized as a religious or faith-based work. I am simply leveraging various sources from different texts building my case.

Quotes By Dr. Alexandra Elinsky

"You can live your dreams, or you can watch them die."

"If you have a problem with feminism, then you are the reason feminism exists."

"Not healing is not an option."

"I look like a lady but act like a man; I've got the best of both worlds in the palm of my hand."

"I would rather die alone having achieved all my dreams than be in a pretend relationship watching them all be stripped away one by one – I want to go to my grave knowing I had more audacity than insecurity hanging onto something that made me less and not more human."

"If I could give one thing to every woman, it would be a pair of balls."

Chapter 1
Big Queen Energy

"You are extremely powerful; your power has no limits."

"If you realized how powerful your thoughts are, you would never think a negative thought" – Peace Pilgrim.

*A note from Dr. Elinsky: It is suggested that you play soothing instrumental music as you read this book for enhanced **healing and relaxation.** Open your mind and receive the learning.*

*"It is 2025, we are dismantling all double standards and bullshit. If we want an equal world, we need equal rules. We will not sit back and be **gluttons for punishment** while certain privileges are given to one gender over another. We are all full human beings."*

As I lay there in the deepest and darkest pits of despair on the hospital bed, I think not of my unfortunate circumstances, not of my pain, suffering, Depression, and anxiety, **but instead, I envision the beautiful, almost dream-like life I will live someday. The life I am living today.** The only thing standing in my way from realizing my life's beauty was time… **for in time, all dreams and desires come true, and pain will be no more…** pain is cast **into the seas of yesterday, never to be remembered again.**

Always remember, all things happen in due course.

Do you value and respect yourself? Stop for a minute and really think about this question. Lay down and reflect on it for as long as you need to. **I have been told that women do not want respect, that they only want love, and that is bullshit.** Every human being needs to be valued and respected no matter who they are or where they come from. **Respect says, "I am a human being; you are a human being. Let's treat each other like human beings."**

Oftentimes, amongst my family, friends, and clients, I notice disturbing patterns of behavior; *people are always lessening themselves.* I call this behavior **THE GREAT SUPPRESSION.** I get it. You want to be humble. You do not want to come across as haughty and arrogant. **You think by continuously lowering your value, you will garner the respect of others, but the reverse is true.** People follow you. *If you lower yourself, they will also lower you. But if you raise yourself up, others will also raise you up.* This is why being humble can often serve more as a self-sabotage than a trait of virtue.

Guys are On Your Side

Men are **more likely** to value women who value themselves. Men are more likely to respect women who respect themselves. **Men love women who love themselves.** If you cannot give love, value, respect, and worth to yourself, then it will be **IMPOSSIBLE** for others to give it to you. What I am arguing is something called **INTERNAL VALIDATION**. There is not one person in this world who does not chase **EXTERNAL VALIDATION** to a greater or lesser degree.

External Validation makes all of us feel good about ourselves; it is the fuel we need to sustain our egos and our own worthiness; however, we get in trouble by constantly seeking that *external validation. We end up chasing it, and whatever we chase runs away from us.* That is the law of human nature. The solution? *Stop chasing external validation. External validation is and should be* <u>**ONLY A BONUS**</u>. This means that when you get it, which you will from time to time, it is a bonus for you. *External validation should never ever be the anchor that holds you psychologically together.*

Cancel Your Ego

The most powerful thing you can do is **to cancel your ego.** It is far easier said than done, but the idea is to transcend your ego *aiming for higher levels of spirituality and consciousness.* If you can move away from a self-centered focus plagued by desire and pleasure, you can reach greater *ascension* within yourself. This is not a process that can be done overnight as it requires significant amounts of *self-discipline.* If you stop fixating on the highs of whatever your fixes are (sex, love, shopping, drugs, alcohol, gossip, money, fame, etc.), then simply by *letting go* of such earthly pleasures, by *cancelling your ego*, you will naturally begin to magnetize yourself attracting these things to you organically without any effort at all. You will attract such things as love, sex, amazing relationships, money, fame, wealth, health, abundance, creativity, more intelligence, greater intuition, and all other *spiritual gifts.*

How to Cancel Your Ego

STEP 1: Meditate daily (2-3 times per day for 10-30 minutes is recommended).
STEP 2: Remove all stressors and blockages.
STEP 3: Remove all negativity and toxic people from your life.
STEP 4: Always educate yourself and read more.
STEP 5: Learn to let go and heal.

Let go of EVERYTHING. LEARN TO LOOSEN THE GRIPS. People tend to hold onto their past no matter how traumatic it might have been for them. Holding on to the past, in a sense, can be comforting as you relive the trauma repeatedly. This is unhealthy and unproductive behavior. The past no longer exists. It is only in your head. All you have is the **present moment**. The future does not even exist (it will exist in the future). This is why we must learn to live now and *go with the flow.* Planning is not always necessary. Plans never go 100% according to planning. *Planning, therefore, is stressful and unproductive.* For example, a vacation. Vacations are typically planned moment by moment and hour by hour. That is stressful and not fun. *It causes rushing around instead of living in and enjoying each moment for what it is and not what you want it to be.*

Common things to let go of:

1. Planning
2. Perfectionism
3. The past
4. Mistakes
5. Trauma
6. Painful memories
7. Control
8. Insecurities
9. Doubts
10. Fears
11. Unwanted emotions and thoughts

Say this out loud now – I release it, I release it, I release it.

Then… think about what you want. **Think about what you want to RECEIVE.**

Then say this out loud now – I receive it, I receive it, I receive it.

You are meant to have EXACTLY what you want to have.

Because that is the definition of I AM.

Learn to validate internally every day. In mastering this skill, you will revolutionize your life, and you will begin to magnetically draw people closer to you, thereby rendering a greater return on external validation. External validation can only come naturally and not by force. This is why asking someone if you look pretty does not work. Let them tell you that you look pretty without you asking. Understand that everything comes and goes through you, **and you have 100% power and control over your life.** We are all told that we do not have any power and that we are powerless. That is bullshit. You have massive amounts of power, uncapped ability, and limitless potential. **By keeping women pregnant, caretakers, and in the kitchen, society has systemically placed us into roles carefully defined and constructed to keep us from changing the world.**

In most cases, a preoccupied and busy mother does not have time to fully and completely chase her little-girl-dreams, but isn't it funny how this reality never seems to impact men in the same way? *Men are always allowed to be whoever they want to be, screw up without consequence, and f*ck as much as they want without being thought of as a slut. As women, we are naturally punished for crimes we did not commit. Endlessly shamed and blamed, <u>we are the ultimate scapegoats of society.</u>*

They have warped us into believing we are nothing and that if we don't find love and get married, we will die alone. *Sisters, it is time to wake TF up. We live in a world where we must be stronger than ever before because we cannot rely on anyone anymore except for ourselves. <u>Appoint yourself the Queen of your life.</u>* See and understand yourself as royalty and treat yourself as such. *You need Big Queen Energy.*

This is an infectious energy that people naturally gravitate to. There will be an irresistible allure about you, and you will draw people to you like a *magnetic force*. You deserve everything you want to have and then some. You do not need to struggle forever, but you should understand you are in the driver's seat here. Many of you have been sitting as passengers for much of your life, and it is not serving you. Go put a crown on your head and start walking around like you are a Queen. Treat yourself like a Queen. *Give yourself the love, respect, adoration, and admiration you wish you could get from others, and then watch how others naturally follow your behaviors.* In his book, *The Spontaneous Fulfillment of Desire*, Deepak Chopra says, "There are two kinds of power that emanate from the self. The first is the power of agency – the power that comes from having a famous name, lots of money, or an impressive title. The power of agency can be formidable, but it eventually comes to an end. True power comes from within, and it has a spiritual rather than a material foundation. It is permanent and does not die with your body. With agency, identity and power come from some external reference object, a situation, a status symbol, a relationship, and money. With self-power, identity comes from listening to the true self, and power comes from the internal reference of spirit. When you work from this internal reference, your sense of self is clear and is not affected by external factors. This is the source of personal power. When external factors fail to influence your sense of self, you become immune to criticism or praise. You also understand that we are all equal because we are all connected to the same conscious intelligence flow. That means that you understand that as you move through your life, you are beneath no one and superior to no one. You don't have to beg or plead or convince anyone of anything because you don't have to convince yourself."

Selfishness and Narcissism

The scapegoat is forever a vessel of sacrifice. She is the definition of selflessness, hardly existing at all. Being nothing but a servant to all those around who act helplessly to receive undeserved benefits and rewards. **No one is helpless.** *They only act helplessly to get you to bow down and worship their every whim and need.* **They are expert takers.** *And the scapegoat (you) is an expert-giver. But the tables are turning, baby!*

At its core, Narcissism is selfishness or extreme love for the self at the expense of others. Everyone is selfish. You cannot be a human without being selfish because selfishness comes with it — **an awareness of and preservation of the self.** Men are conditioned to become fixated on themselves, so you see many men become Narcissists. Women are conditioned to become fixated on others, so you see many women become empaths. **That does not mean the reverse can't be true.** Of course, there are narcissistic women and empathic men, but I am speaking of a **worldwide pattern** here that each of you has noticed to a greater or lesser degree.

The solution is to harmonize balance, knowing how to receive but also willing to give. Some people are all Narcissists, and that is not good. Others are all empaths, and that is not good. Learn to strike this perfect balance between Narcissism and empathy if you are to thrive and survive in this world. *Learn to balance yourself out.* If you lean more toward empath, then start to become more focused on yourself. If you lean more toward narcissistic traits, then begin to become more empathic and *emotionally aware* of others. *You cannot take care of others at your own expense. You cannot wipe someone else's ass if you have not wiped your own ass first.*

The Universal Wiping of Asses

Women are so conditioned into the empath role that it has made many of us *gluttons for punishment*; I know because I used to be one. *I thought the more I loved, gave, did, and cared, the more it would be reciprocated back, and it was not.* So, I did the reverse. I stopped loving, giving, doing, and caring so hard, and as a result, I received more love, doing, and caring coming my way. *Reverse psychology at its best.* This is why if you really like a guy, don't do shit for him. *He will appreciate you far more.* Let him bow down and worship you for once. In many relationships, the woman is bowing down and worshipping the man while he is walking all over her, but if she can learn to stop that shit, he will begin to do the worshipping. *Remember ladies, if you bow down and worship someone, they will walk all over you.* This is why you need *Big Queen Energy*. This is why being selfish is not as bad as you think it is. *You were just conditioned to believe selfishness is a terrible thing, yet men have been doing it for years, and no one has said anything to them about it. I am fully convinced that being and acting like a woman simply does not work. Men are outstanding role models. Kudos to you, men; we can all take notes from you.*

Life Purpose

I do not know who needs to hear this, but if you sit down and really think about it, you were not put on this earth to date, get married, have sex, or make babies. Yes, sex and babies keep our species alive, so we must reproduce keeping humanity going long-term. However, the purpose of your personhood does not revolve around reproduction; it is only an extension of it. Meaning, sure, go have sex and reproduce, but don't believe that is the only reason why you are breathing. We have convinced women (by glamorizing marriage and pregnancy) that getting married and becoming a mother is the most important thing a woman can do. It is not. Robert Greene, in *The Concise Laws of Human Nature*, dissertates, "With a sense of purpose, we feel much less insecure. We have an overall sense that we are advancing, realizing some or all our potential. We can begin to look back at various accomplishments, small or large. We know who we are, and this self-awareness becomes our anchor in life."

If you have not tapped into your **Life Purpose** already, please do so now. Really dig deep and uncover whatever it is you find true meaning and joy in. What do you like doing? What makes you feel good? **What types of activities give you the emotions you WANT to feel?** Some of you know what your life purpose is, and some of you do not, and if you do not, it is okay. You do not always have to have it all figured out. Life takes time to master as we are continuously navigating murky waters, trying, failing, and picking ourselves up as we go. Your life is a timeline. You are born, you grow up, you become an adult, you live your adult life, you age, and then you eventually die. **What is between birth and death is your life.** Life is what you make of it. You can do anything you want. Never let a person, place, thing, or situation hold you back. **You were put here to do something great and make some big difference in enhancing the lives of others.** Use your time and talents wisely.

The Big Conundrum – Love Versus Potentiality Versus Possibility

I am not someone who has many regrets in life, but I do have one, and it is colossal. Once upon a time, back when I was a *glutton for punishment, I gave up my dreams for love.* Someone who I thought loved and cherished me forced me mercilessly to give up my dreams, my little girl dreams, and I did. The good news is I did not go down without a fight, but I did go down, and I eventually conceded, which is the saddest thing I have ever done. Why did I do this? *Because, at the time, my need for love and security was greater than my need for potentiality. And I was willing to risk and sacrifice my innate human potential for what turned out to be breadcrumbs of love at best and, at worst, a failed relationship.* Digging deeper, it was not even the love I really wanted. *It was my need for security. My need to matter. My need to be seen, heard, and listened to.* Please understand there is no security in this world. *You can only become secure through insecurity. Your insecurities are what propels you to security. That is why you must face them head-on. There is no easier way to do this.*

I gave up my dreams for love, and to this very day, that regret is eating me alive. Every single one of us has been lied to since the day we were born. We are fed all this bullshit about love, happily ever after, one day your prince will come, love will rescue you, marriage, family, babies, and truthfully, I hate being so abrasive here, *but it is all one big giant crock of shit. There is no prince charming, no happily ever after, love won't rescue you, being alone won't kill you, and raising kids is nothing but hard work, self-sacrifice, and stress. That is the f*cking truth.* But they lied to you. Why? Because those who raised them lied to them, too. *They want you believing in love so that you will never become anything*—so that you will not ever rise to the f*cking top. So that you will remain stuck, unhappy, freaked out, lonely, sad, depressed, and anxious until you die. What a life!

Are there happy marriages and families in the world? The answer is yes; of course there are! But it takes **TWO PEOPLE** to want that, build that, and do that together, completely moving in the *same direction.* Let me tell you something, okay? *In over 90% of cases, marriage counseling does not work, and do you want to know why?* **Because in those 90% of cases, more than** *likely, one partner is a Narcissist, and the other is an empath. The empath wants to work on and "fix" the marriage. They want things to get better. They will do anything to enhance, fix, and optimize the relationship. The Narcissist, on the other hand, because they are only about themselves and not about the totality of the relationship, DOES NOT want to fix the relationship. If the relationship were to actually get better and become "fixed," that would mean that the Narcissist would not be allowed to be a Narcissist anymore. The Narcissist would "lose all of the benefits" that they naturally gain from being a Narcissist and having that level of complete power and control over the relationship.*

How can marriage counseling work when one partner refuses to change? It cannot. Now you know why over 50% of marriages end in divorce, and of the other 50%, 25% or more of those unhappy partners are being **gluttons for punishment.** It is one thing to be a glutton for punishment for a decade, but a lifetime of living like that is another story. Narcissists are so grossly and inherently selfish and completely emotionally stunted **(emotional infantilism)** that they are literally **too brainless (emotionally unaware)** to even have the cognition that YOU (the other person) even matter in the relationship at all. **Your emotional needs deserve to be met, and if they aren't, then consider yourself a glutton for punishment.**

How does someone become a Narcissist and how does someone become an empath? In the same way one person becomes lazy while another person becomes driven and successful – **the difference is social conditioning.** What is social conditioning? **Social conditioning, in simple terms, refers to how you were raised.** It is the social, physical, and emotional environment in which you were raised. The **subconscious mind** takes all words and teachings at **face value. What that means is whatever you were taught, you will believe.** Read that again – **whatever you were taught, you will believe.** This is why words carry so much power. The subconscious mind cannot understand a negative. This is why humans victimize themselves; they believe in their own thoughts. They convince themselves of things that are or are not true. The only thing that matters is what you believe. **You literally are your beliefs.** This is why the way kids are raised scares the shit out of me. We grow up so messed up to a greater or lesser degree. The world is so messed up and everyone is suffering incessantly, barely getting by many of us. *We all have the power to be far happier and fulfilled, but because of this social conditioning, many of us remain stuck forever until we die, never living the life we were put on this earth to live.*

The Narcissistic Family

I researched the **Narcissistic Family.** What amazes me is how Narcissistic families are so textbook. The Narcissistic parent(s) assign certain roles to certain children, and the big three roles are the following: **The Golden Child (spoiled and can do no wrong), The Invisible Child (neglected), and The Scapegoat (takes on the blame and shame of the family and is bullied by parents and other siblings).** In some families, not all, because male children historically have been more desirous than female children, it is not uncommon for the male child to be the Golden or spoiled child, and the female child becomes **the scapegoat or good girl** (taking on the family blame and shame). Because the male Golden Child is allowed a self, he grows up becoming a Narcissist too because, after all, the world has always revolved around him, hasn't it? And the female Scapegoat grows up becoming the **glutton for punishment** because Eve ate the apple first, didn't she? **The Scapegoat becomes the unworthy, insecure girl who struggles with Depression and Anxiety her whole life, which is statistically more common for women than men, is it not?**

These assigned roles have the audacity to play out in our romantic relationships, whereas the man remains the Narcissist or abuser (claiming all the rewards and glory as he did as the

Golden Child) while the woman Scapegoat becomes a Co-Dependent sucker craving the **constant validation and love** she never received as a child only for her Narcissistic husband to endlessly punish her for all eternity just as her parents did before him. She is familiar with the Narcissist and thus forms a trauma bond with him. ***She is never good enough or worthy on her own, which makes it impossible for her to validate internally.*** She has been suppressed her entire life, and she doesn't know happiness or abundance the way her Narcissistic husband knows it. ***<u>Why all this suffering for the scapegoat? Oh, that is right, simply because of her gender and no other criteria at all.</u>***

All the Scapegoat's power has been dismantled by her parents and spouse until she finally heals and unleashes **THE INSURMOUNTABLE POWER DEEP WITHIN HER. *She is THE ESCAPEGOAT- SHE IS THE G.O.A.T – THE GREATEST OF ALL TIME!***

BLESSED IS THE SCAPEGOAT – FOR THE ENTIRE WORLD BELONGS TO HER.

Everyone makes such a big deal out of marriage, but in so many countless cases, it is the marriage that is killing our self-esteem. We end up with unhealed, unresourceful, lazy, ill-intentioned, controlling jerks proving to us repeatedly how unworthy we are. Since your **subconscious mind** takes everything at face value, **what do you think will happen?** That is right; you have become **less human. For the love of God, please understand that your self-esteem and self-worth are not up for grabs, damnit.** This brings me to my next point.

Here is a quick nugget – **do you want to know how to easily make someone so completely obsessed and captivated by you?**

The answer – <u>never give all of yourself to that person.</u> What is rare and given in small dosages is seen as highly magnetic, irresistible, prize-worthy, and desirous.

Like your parents ignoring you as a child but then trying to be buddy-buddy when you are a busy adult and now you have no time for them – ironic, isn't it? **Familiarity breeds contempt and absence does make the heart grow fonder.**

Your problem is that you give way too much to your man and then wonder why he doesn't love you. The definition of insanity is... well, you know the definition of insanity. **<u>This is why transformation is not optional. It is necessary.</u>**

Normal Life goes 100% against Human Nature.

Let me define **a normal life** *– this normal life is what most people do – they are born, they are kids, they go to school, they go to college or get a job, they get married, they settle down, they have kids, they raise kids, they retire, and then they die. That is their life.* <u>*That is a normal life.*</u> **THAT IS NOT WHAT YOU WERE PUT ON THIS EARTH TO DO.**

Why are you even here? Have you ever asked yourself that question? The meaning of life question. What is my purpose? If you have not, you do have a purpose, and it is not just to push out kids managing endless laundry, dishes, and temper tantrums; you're not a maid.

Ask yourself – **what do I want?** I have met many women who "all they want" is to get married and have kids. Okay, cool, I get it. I am not trying to negate or belittle that at all, but the question is, is that all? Is that really all? Do you really want that, or is that what you were told you want? I see so many people walk around miserable, unhappy, unhealed, complaining, gossiping, belittling, settling, unproductive, loathing, and negative, and it really makes me wonder... **they are not doing what they were put on this earth to do because if they did, they wouldn't be feeling the way that they feel inside.**

Exploring Our Emotional Worlds

The one thing that makes all of us human is our emotions. Every person has what I call an **emotional world**, and your **emotional world** is made up of your emotions. Your **emotional world** is an amalgamation of high highs, low lows, and everything in between. It is comprised of feel-good emotions, feel-bad emotions, and neutral emotions. You feel all the time. There is not a second that goes by when you are not in an emotional state. Even if you feel more neutral or bored, well, bored is still a feeling. Remember, from *GIRL GAME: BALLS OUT,* all emotions are on a spectrum of significance. The high highs or *feel good emotions* are what I refer to as *heaven states* because if given a choice, all of us would select to always feel heaven states. The low lows or *feel bad emotions* are called *hell states*. Another term I use for hell states is the *Abyss of Misery.* More neutral or non-emotionally charged emotions are called *purgatory states.* I advise everyone to remain in purgatory or *calm states* as often as possible. *I recommend this because high highs or feel good emotions do not last forever.* Usually, after a high or feel good state, most people experience a plummet or let-down where they are cast back into hell. We never recommend going from heaven to hell, which happens often. You want to go from heaven into purgatory. And similarly, it is better to be in purgatory than hell. If you are in a hell state, the idea is to get you back into purgatory as quickly as possible so that you do not remain in the hell state for long.

Pay closer attention to your *emotional world* and watch as your emotions tend to swing back and forth often from hell to heaven, heaven to hell, purgatory to heaven, hell to purgatory, and so on... *what we are experiencing in our lives at any given moment will determine where we stand on the emotional spectrum.* Peace is the only emotion that truly matters; this means that all emotions are positive (even so-called hell states) because it is GOOD for you to feel even if you are in hell (and I understand you never want to be in hell. I get it, trust me) but nonetheless you need to feel deeply experiencing hell states from time to time hopefully not long-term. ***The fact that you feel intensely is what makes you human; do not shy away from your feelings.***

The Emotional Scale

We are going to do a deep dive into emotions and learn about the *Emotional Guidance Scale* developed by Esther Hicks / Abraham-Hicks Emotional Guidance Scale. The *Emotional Guidance Scale* is a way to perceive emotions. The scale helps us understand and navigate our emotions so that we can learn how to acquire and maintain high vibrational frequencies attracting positive experiences and abundance into our lives. The underlying idea is that we can CHOOSE and CHANGE our THOUGHTS, and when we influence our thoughts, our emotions naturally change. *In other words, we can choose our emotions, and we can choose to FEEL GOOD (heaven states) all the time! How amazing is that?*

The *Emotional Guidance Scale* is a scale of positive or high-vibration emotions and negative or low-vibration emotions. A person can move either up or down the scale.

The Emotional Guidance Scale

1. Joy / Appreciation / Empowerment / Freedom / Love
2. Passion
3. Enthusiasm / Eagerness / Happiness
4. Positive Expectation / Belief
5. Optimism
6. Hopefulness
7. Satisfaction / Contentment
8. Boredom
9. Pessimism
10. Frustration / Irritation / Impatience
11. Overwhelm
12. Disappointment
13. Doubt
14. Worry
15. Blame
16. Discouragement
17. Anger

18. Revenge
19. Hatred / Rage
20. Jealousy
21. Insecurity / Guilt / Unworthiness
22. Fear / Grief / Depression / Despair / Powerlessness

1-7 are positive or *wanted emotions,* 8 is neutral emotion and 9-22 are negative or *unwanted emotions.* Your thoughts (which create emotions) can move you up or down the scale at any given time, depending on the situation and circumstances around you. The higher you go on the scale, the better you will feel. For example, Anger, according to this scale, is a better emotion than sadness. It is better to be angry than sad. Any movement up the scale, even by one number, is an improvement in your mood. There is something very important I want to address. **Notice how THE GREATEST EMOTION is EMPOWERMENT, or what we could call powerfulness, and THE LOWEST EMOTION is DISEMPOWERMENT, or what we could call powerlessness. If you are not POWERFUL, you are POWERLESS.** Stop and think about that for a moment. Are you feeling empowered? Are you feeling powerful or disempowered?

For most of my life, I have felt disempowered and powerless, and with that came severe Depression and despair, which I often talk about in my writing. I talk a lot about pain because most of my life to date has been incredibly painful, and most of those associated emotions have been unwanted. **But now, the tables have completely turned.** Right now, I feel **EMPOWERED** and **POWERFUL**, always, every second, minute, and hour of the day. How can that be possible? *I changed my thoughts and therefore, changed my emotions.*

When I was feeling bad and vibrating from low vibrational emotions (unworthiness), I was attracting nothing but sorrow, tough times, difficulties, abuse, disease, and other negative toxic energies into my life from other people. *My life was plagued by unworthiness.* I was operating from a place of worriedness and woundedness and not worthiness. The narrative needed to change. Once I learned about the *Emotional Scale*, I learned that *I HELD THE POWER TO CHANGE MY EMOTIONS* and thus changed my reality, literally becoming the **CREATOR** in my life. *Since we were created, we have THE CREATOR'S POWER.* Make no mistakes about this. It is 100% true. The craziest things happen to me now (the good kind of crazy). I win awards that I don't apply for, and people put me on the cover of their magazines. I get asked to speak at events. My friends are lovely and wonderful. Every guy chase and spoils me (no exaggeration), my clients love me, people respect me, I repel negative energy and forces, I ask for things and get them, I receive random gifts, etc.

When you are vibrating HIGHER, you ATTRACT more. You ATTRACT what you ARE. This is called *The Law of Attraction*. The *Law of Attraction* works off two extremely powerful forces of nature: #1 (Love) and #2 (Emotions). Love is the force of life. Everything we do comes from a place of LOVE. I authored this book series out of a place of LOVE. PURE LOVE. When I started writing **GIRL GRIT: SAVAGE NOT AVERAGE**, I had an idea and just started putting pen to paper for SHITS & GIGGLES. I did not intend to be a serious author at that point in time. I was simply writing my first book. I did it with so much love and passion in my heart. When I wrote it, information would flow out from my typing hands like a hurricane. I never had writer's block. I could write for eight to ten hours straight with no breaks other than to use the restroom. My *Third Eye* was fully activated and the ideas and information flowed. It was **DIVINE INSPIRATION,** all writing is. I wrote from a place of love. *I wrote because I wanted to just write something f*cking real.* I wrote because I knew I was not the only person who felt the way I felt. I wrote because I wanted to help women learn how to suffer less. I am writing because I love every single one of my readers, including you. Can you feel my love right now? Pouring out from these pages?

The second life force is **EMOTION.** Many people feel like shit, which is entirely unnecessary 100% of the time. You should not feel bad ever, and if you do, you will be attracted to negativity because you FEEL NEGATIVE. Do it. Change your **emotional state**, even just for shits and giggles, and notice if anything changes, and you begin to magnetically draw everything to you that you ever dreamed of. ***You can have anything you want, but you must FEEL it first.***

Peace

Peace is the best emotion. People chase and pursue happiness. Happiness is an emotion and not a thing, therefore cannot be achieved or sustained. ***Yes, you can experience feelings of happiness because happiness is a feeling. However, it is not a feeling that typically lasts very long; it is foolish to pursue or chase happiness.*** Similarly, it is foolish to pursue or chase pleasure. You have heard it said that we chase pleasure and run away from pain. This is true. We do that every day of our lives. However, pleasure and pain are never sustainable. Yes, you can achieve pleasure and pain, but both realities cannot be sustained in and of themselves.

You will experience moments of pleasure and moments of pain at contrasting times in your life. Pain does not last forever and neither does pleasure. This is also why it is foolish to chase pleasure; you cannot sustain it. No two experiences will ever be the same. This is why all addiction is bad. Addicts are far more addicted to the chasing of pleasure than the actual pleasure itself. The pleasure itself is far less pleasurable than the pleasure derived from the chase. Peace is paramount. ***You cannot chase peace, but you can achieve peace, and once achieved, you can sustain it. However, it does take work, and it's not an easy task.*** Remain in peace or what I call a **purgatory state** 90% of the time. I suggest 90% because you should allow some time (10%) to experience those heaven and hell emotions. I caution you because those high highs do not last long and will cast you back into the **Abyss of Misery** during the crash phase of the pleasure experience.

Sister – You are BIG QUEEN ENERGY.

Chapter 1 Takeaways

- ➢ Stop chasing **external validation;** learn how to validate internally. **When you validate internally, external validation will be magnetically attracted to you.**
- ➢ Cancel your ego. Let go of the need to control. Loosen the grips opening yourself to receive.
- ➢ Narcissism is a reality we must deal with. Learn to strike a harmonious balance between giving and taking.
- ➢ Pay more attention to your **emotional world** and **emotional states.** Develop a deep awareness of emotion in yourself and others, building your **emotional intelligence.**
- ➢ **Peace is the best emotion.**
- ➢ Empowerment is the highest emotion.
- ➢ Empowerment is the opposite of disempowerment.
- ➢ **There is no such thing as Depression, only disempowerment.**

Share Your Story:

In the space provided, it is time to share your story. How will you develop your **Big Queen Energy** using it to empower yourself?

Chapter 2
Hot Shit

"When she walks into the room, all heads turn, and a pin drops to the floor!"

"All things are subject to interpretation whichever interpretation prevails at a given time is a function of power and not truth" – Friedrich Nietzsche

One of my executive clients was working toward becoming a Chief Executive Officer. I coached her on building **confidence** and **executive presence.** I have zero recollection of telling her that she should walk around like she is **Hot Shit**. According to her, those very words came out of my mouth. I told her to walk around like she is **Hot Shit**. I don't believe I would ever say something like this to an executive, but then again, I have zero filters sometimes. She loved it! She embodied thinking of herself as **Hot Shit**, which is what I wanted for her.

Understand what you think of yourself; other people will think of you. If you think of yourself as being **Hot Shit,** then other people will also think of you as **Hot Shit. Hot Shit** means unusually good. It is a person who is attractive, well-liked, popular, powerful, confident, and charismatic. **People tend to think of themselves as either dwarfs or giants.** You might pivot depending on the situation and circumstances. For example, you could be a giant at work and a dwarf at home or a giant at home and a dwarf at work. **Always perceive yourself as a giant in all circumstances and situations. A giant is Hot Shit;** a dwarf is not. This does not mean you have to become egotistical, but it does not do you any good to have such a low opinion of yourself. **If you hold a low opinion of yourself, then other people will also hold a low opinion of you.**

In all my years of study and research, I am most convinced that someone who regards themselves as **Hot Shit** while remaining humble and sensitive to others' feelings and needs will:

- ➢ Never be rejected (romantically and otherwise)
- ➢ Will have more friends
- ➢ More romantic interests and options
- ➢ Better moods
- ➢ Higher quality of life
- ➢ Greater opportunities
- ➢ Make more money
- ➢ Feel worthy and good enough
- ➢ Mitigate feelings of failure and inadequacy
- ➢ Attract good things into their lives

It is advantageous to think highly versus lowly of yourself. **Keep in mind I am not encouraging Narcissism or ego. There is balance and harmony to every reality. <u>I am advocating for mindful self-esteem.</u>** You can think highly of yourself while remaining humble. In the same respect, if you are mindful, sensitive, and aware of others and their thoughts, feelings, opinions, and needs, you will be fine. **A true Narcissist has no social awareness of others.** This is due to their lack of empathy. **However, suppose you remain empathic while highly valuing yourself. In that case, you subconsciously place a higher value on yourself, which in turn subconsciously programs others also to give you a high opinion in their regard of you.** What you are doing is **lifting yourself.** As you lift yourself up, you lift others. When you lift others with you, you will notice that **EVERYBODY WINS. <u>This is called EMPOWERMENT.</u>**

...

My sister is not one to give anyone any compliments, so if you happen to get a compliment from her, she really means it. On Thanksgiving Day, 2024, we went out for a holiday dinner. She noticed me walking back to our table from the restroom. She watched me confidently walk back to the family dinner table.

Once I sat down, she told me how she noticed other people looking at and admiring me as I walked, something I failed to notice. She proceeds to say, *"Alex, when you walk into the room, you command everyone to attention at once; all heads turn, and a pin drops to the floor!"* A pin drops, really!? Wow! After she gave her compliment, she jerked her head sharply to one side, physically demonstrating how fast heads turn when I enter a room. It was funny and I was flattered. I didn't know I turned heads, commanded attention, and even caused pins to drop to the floor.

This is that powerful executive presence! I dress to impress everywhere I go. I am a fashionista put together from head to toe. Hair is perfectly styled, makeup and face flawless, nails done, and color-coordinated outfits with various styles and patterns perfectly blended creating *a striking and captivating appearance.* My students used to tell me I could dress my ass off. I usually wear multiple layers and always accessorize. I create any kind of look with a simple or extravagant wardrobe. ***How you look is how you feel.***

I live in Cleveland, Ohio; most people here only wear jeans, sweats, and hoodies, even to nicer establishments. Even when I am dressed down, I am dressed up compared to most Ohioans. I wish people took more pride in their appearances. Some women are plain when it comes to dress. You don't have to be a plain Jane if you don't want to. How are you supposed to turn heads and command attention if you look exactly like the next girl? You are supposed to be **Hot Shit. *If you want to manifest a million bucks, then dress like a million bucks.*** You can look rich even if you aren't rich.

Fashion is important in all situations and settings, from work to social outings. When it comes to apparel, I suggest always using layers and accessorizing. Your outfit should make a statement. Tights complement skirts and dresses beautifully. Pants can be colored and styled appearing trendy and fashionable. Hats are powerful and should be worn more often, along with belts. Use lots of colors ensuring they coordinate well. Dress for the seasons and think of naming your looks to match the feel. *Be extra if you want.*

Command attention with your style, posture, facial expressions and gestures, words, the way you speak, how you move, and how you think and feel. No more hiding from the world. No more being another compliant girl. *Compliance is for the shy and average woman without the desire to ascend.*

The Mary Poppins Effect

You might be familiar with the story of Mary Poppins. Upon studying this film as an adult, I find Mary Poppin's behavior and demeanor fascinating as it relates to confidence and power. *Everything Mary Poppins touches turns to gold.* I noticed how, upon her arrival at the Banks home, she confidently lets herself into the home, walking right up to Mr. Banks with a *self-assuredness* I do not see in most people. Poised, confident, controlled, and well-spoken, Mary Poppins sells herself to Mr. Banks as to why she is the right fit for the nanny position. I admired how confidently she carries herself, as this is not a disposition I find in many women. Looking perplexed, Mr. Banks doesn't know what hit him and Mary Poppins practically hires herself.

She proceeds upstairs, visiting the children amazing them with her wit, intelligence, and firmness. Her no-nonsense approach has the children commanded at attention. They are mesmerized by her and all that she is capable of. They ran all over the previous nanny; well, there is no running over Mary Poppins.

Everyone knows her name and they say it often because Mary Poppins is important. She is treasured, admired, and respected. *Don't you want to be respected everywhere you go?* Everyone falls at her feet, and she gets lots of complimentary things. *I asked myself what it was about Mary Poppins that could command such attention from all. I have learned that if you (act) like a Queen, people will treat you like one.* Then it hit me. Mary Poppins (acts) like and carries herself as a **Confident, Resilient, No-nonsense Queen,** and people fall at her feet! Because she carries herself with confidence, grace, and assuredness, everyone around her follows. Mary Poppins is a powerful woman, turning heads and commanding attention everywhere she goes. It's in the way she dresses, talks, carries herself, behaves, relates, understands, and listens; it's her mind and her wit, her humor, her imagination – everything about her is magic because she ACTS like a Queen!

Go watch this movie, or if you've seen it as a child, watch it now as an adult. It is an entirely different experience watching a movie as an adult compared to when you were a child. The movie hit me so differently as an adult because I was studying Mary and her behavior.

In my coaching observations, many women are depressed and lack confidence. Heads hang low; people are burdened and stressed, defeated, and sad. **You've got to perceive yourself as the giant and not the dwarf.** You've got to perceive yourself as **Hot Shit.** You've got to perceive yourself as Mary Poppins. You've got to think highly of yourself as a **Resilient Goddess Queen.**

This life can be demeaning. Everything will eat you alive if you don't take a stand for your **self-esteem** right now. In *The 48 Laws of Power*, Robert Greene discusses garnering attention, "Burning more brightly than those around you is a skill no one is born with. You must learn to attract attention. At the start of your career, you must attach your name and reputation to a quality, an image that sets you apart from other people. This image can be something like a characteristic style of dress or a personality quirk that amuses people and gets talked about. Once the image is established, you have an appearance, a place in the sky for your star. It is a common mistake to imagine that this peculiar appearance of yours should not be controversial, that to be attacked is somehow bad. Nothing could be farther from the truth. To avoid being a flash in the pan and having your notoriety eclipsed by another, you must not discriminate between different types of attention; in the end, every kind will work in your favor."

The Beauty of Sexiness

I am so sick and tired of all the sex-shaming women have endured growing up. The double standards, the purity talk, slut-shaming, etc. ***We are allowed to be sexual beings because we are sexual beings.*** Humanity has skewed sex. We have made it wrong and dirty through perception when, in fact, it is not. It is a natural part of life. You were created to be sexy, to feel sexy, and to embrace your internal and external sexiness. Humans are sexual beings. We should revel in our authentic sexiness.

Do this activity now. Put on some sexy lingerie, play some romantic or sensual music, and dance in front of your full-body mirror, admiring your sexy body and sexuality. Do this alone with no one around. ***Love yourself and your sexy body.***

You have been subconsciously programmed since childhood to be thin, not to eat much, to starve yourself, to throw up your food, and to exercise like crazy. You have been body shamed. Your mom, grandma, and aunt told you all these sayings about beauty being associated with thinness. You have become programmed to be obsessed with your weight sometimes to the point of eating disorders. ***Learn to appreciate and accept your body just as it is.*** I do not care if you are 500 pounds. You can still love your body just as you are. ***You can reprogram your mind to love your body instead of despising it.***

I received more male attention weighing 250 lbs. versus 150 lbs. because at 250 lbs. I was far more confident and self-assured. That was all that mattered to guys. They did not really know the difference between 150 and 250. I was not treated differently for being more overweight; in fact, they all loved my curves. I had no problem getting attention, dates, love, affection, gifts, etc., because I was so confident. I was glowing, happy, vivacious, and joyful. *I was not complaining about my body or weight in front of them and putting myself down.*

Remember, what we think of ourselves is what others will think of us. If you think you are beautiful, sexy, brilliant, and happy just as you are, then you will convince him of that too, and he will share the same beliefs that you hold about yourself. We have been programmed with so much bullshit growing up that has done nothing to advance us as human beings. The message is all the same in girlhood – go to school, go to college or not, get married, have kids, work or not, retire, enjoy your grandkids, and die. *We are programmed to live unfulfilling lives filled with sadness, hard work, and mediocrity.* We mope around feeling arduous about the tasks in front of us because there is always so much to do, and everyone is demanding something from us.

Inspirational Memories + Awe Moments

You feel some kind of emotion every second of your day. *People are chasing emotions.* Similarly, people who use drugs and alcohol are using those to elicit the emotions that drugs and alcohol provide. Your *emotional world* is a significant component of your life. If given the option, you would probably rather experience feel-good versus feel-bad emotions. People do all kinds of crazy things when they experience feel-bad emotions because the goal is to get rid of those feel-bad emotions as quickly as possible replacing them with feel-good emotions.

I cannot speak for you, but my own life seems to be an amalgamation of high and low emotions. This is part of our human experience. Anything can impact how we feel, including people, situations, jobs, thoughts, circumstances, the weather, our pets, moods and, of course, substances. Although I have plenty of highs and happy moments in my life, my life is also not free from strife, struggle, and challenge. No matter where you are in life or how many resources you have access to, more than likely, you will experience challenges at different ages and stages of your life. ***Always embrace challenges and struggles.*** Understand them as friends and not enemies. This will mitigate their power over you. ***<u>Challenges and struggles are strategically placed into your life building your character, forming resilience, and propelling personal growth and ascension.</u>***

Two exercises that can help you replace feel-bad emotions with feel-good emotions are the following:

1. ***Remembering or reliving Happy and Inspirational Memories***
2. ***Remembering Moments of Awe***

Throughout your day, good things will happen to you. A few examples could be but are not limited to:

- ✓ That morning cup of coffee
- ✓ Fresh air
- ✓ Sunshine
- ✓ A carefree drive to work with your favorite music
- ✓ Hot shower
- ✓ An iced coffee
- ✓ Positive reinforcement from your boss or coworkers
- ✓ An exciting email or phone call
- ✓ Some good news
- ✓ A good meal
- ✓ Nice weather
- ✓ A clean and organized home
- ✓ Kids listening
- ✓ A kiss and hug from your significant other
- ✓ An I love you
- ✓ Other positive words and affirmations

Or anything else you can add to this list! These should be *small happy memories* you can reflect on throughout your day, especially during moments of feeling low or feel-bad emotions, extra stress and anxiety. *They will help you pivot your thought processes focusing on all that is going right in your life versus all that is going wrong.* By focusing on small wins throughout the day, such as a hot cup of coffee in the morning or a hot shower, you will regain clarity and focus beginning to chip away at unwanted feel-bad emotions that should not be taking up space in your head. *Additionally, this simple exercise will raise your vibrational level because when you FEEL GOOD, you will attract positive things to you.* You cannot attract when you feel bad. Therefore, it is advantageous to FEEL GOOD as often as possible mitigating feeling bad. *Simple shifts in perspective will have a profound and lasting impact on your daily life.*

Similarly, consider awe-moments. *Awe-moments* instantly raise your emotions and vibrational energies. *An awe-moment is any significant event in your life that creates an awe-inspiring feeling within you.* Some examples include:

- ✓ A job promotion
- ✓ Getting a new job
- ✓ Having a baby
- ✓ Getting married
- ✓ Publishing a book
- ✓ Starting a business
- ✓ Winning an award
- ✓ Making a dream come true
- ✓ Visiting an exotic place
- ✓ A dream vacation
- ✓ Attending an empowering conference
- ✓ Watching a live show
- ✓ Witnessing a miracle
- ✓ A baby's firsts
- ✓ Getting engaged
- ✓ Recognition

✓ Falling in love

These are just a few, but I am sure you have an entire arsenal of *awe-inspiring moments* throughout your life. *Reflect on these often.* You can easily access and elicit those same *strong positive emotions* you felt in the moment of the actual experience. *Do this to raise your emotional and vibrational energies.*

Bubblehead

Laughter is essential for emotional well-being. Laughter is the wellspring of life. Laughter is a release of negative emotional vibrations. *It's shifting from the negative into the positive.* Laughter is good for your soul. I worked at a marketing company when I was 18 years old. My boss was a loud, angry Italian man from New York with a heavy New York accent. He yelled at EVERYONE constantly for any reason or no reason at all. His face was always blood red. He would yell at me, too, and I couldn't help but laugh hysterically in his face. I was laughing because his yelling, red face, and heavy NY accent made me laugh. I couldn't help it. I could not take him seriously. My laughter made him even angrier, as you can imagine. He nicknamed me *Bubblehead* because all I had to do was take one look at him and I would burst into laughter; I honestly couldn't help it.

I saw him yell at us, employees, his clients, stakeholders, and the man delivering the mail – everyone and anyone! I witnessed him chase solicitors down the hallway scaring the innocent away. He was a hoot! I don't know if it was the accent, the red face, or the way he looked at me when he yelled that made me laugh so hard. His most famous quote to anyone was, *"You're busting my balls!"* Say that with a heavy NY accent! Everyone was always busting his balls, supposedly. Especially me, Ms. Bubblehead.

Be a Bubblehead. Don't be so serious. Don't be so grumpy. Lower your expectations. Live more. Laugh more. Find joy in all situations and circumstances.

Sister – You are Hot Shit.

Chapter 2 Takeaways

- ➤ Unworthiness begins with a low opinion of yourself.
- ➤ Perceive yourself as **Hot Shit** and other people will perceive you that way.
- ➤ You can be humble and mindful of other people while still having a healthy and high opinion of yourself. ***This is the essence of mindful self-esteem.***
- ➤ Develop a commanding **executive presence** – turn heads and drop pins with your style, posture, walk, talk, and presence. ***Your aura should be glowing and sparkling.***
- ➤ Study Mary Poppins – her behavior commands attention from everyone she interacts with.
- ➤ ***It is better to be a giant than a dwarf.***
- ➤ Happy **inspirational memories** and **awe-moments** will raise your emotional vibrations attracting all wonderful things into your life.
- ➤ Feeling bad will never serve you well.
- ➤ Laughter also raises your vibrational energies.

Share Your Story:

In the space provided, it is time to share your story. What is unique about you? Think about a time you **commanded attention.** Describe a time when you felt like **Hot Shit**. What did you do that made you feel that way?

Chapter 3
Power

*"If a woman feels worthy in a relationship, but a man does not, she will break up with him. Similarly, if a man feels worthy in a relationship, but a woman does not, he will break up with her. Everything becomes a **self-fulfilling prophecy** because everyone is a mirror or reflection of ourselves. It's impossible for anyone to break up with you because clearly, only you broke up with yourself."*

"To live is to suffer, to survive is to find some meaning in the suffering." – Friedrich Nietzsche

Power

This book is about power; it is about the personal innate power that we as human beings uniquely possess. Most people do not recognize that they have this power; therefore, they feel powerless, but that is simply not true. They just haven't tapped into their power. As someone keen on definitions, ***I believe that power is the ability to do or to act.*** It is our unique capacity to accomplish and achieve. ***Power means capacity.*** If you feel powerless, you are not powerless at all. There is simply something going on inside of you, like a blockage of some sort. Norman Vincent Peale, in *The Power of Positive Thinking*, says this about power, "We have seen the demonstration of atomic energy. We know that astonishing and enormous amounts of energy exist in the universe. This same force of energy is resident in the human mind. Nothing on earth is greater than the human mind in potential power. The average individual is capable of much greater achievement than he has ever realized."

When I think of power, I think of audacity. Audacity is boldness or the confidence to act. Synonyms for audacity are grit and nerve, which is interesting because my first book is titled ***GIRL GRIT: SAVAGE NOT AVERAGE. GIRL GRIT*** is about having the audacity (or grit/nerve) to assume personal power *rising above your pain and circumstances.* People are amazed at people with audacity. *Therefore, audacity is a primary form of power.*

Why We Feel Powerless?

We feel a sense of powerlessness because society loves to suppress us, making us feel smaller than we are. Remember, there is a time and place for humility, but it would not serve you to remain in that state perpetually. *You can be humble while still being powerful.* One of the reasons why I suggest that you read, study, and learn more is because *knowledge is power.* The more you know, the more powerful you will become. Why? **<u>Because competence produces confidence.</u>** The more competent you are, the more confident you will feel. *Become more authentic and braver.* People love storytelling. It is what connects you to an audience. *When you are honest and genuine, people will trust you.* People do not trust fakes and phonies.

Society also limits you and puts you into a box. Go to school, go to college, get a job, buy a house, get married, work, retire, and die. Although these activities can be fulfilling, they limit a lot of people. For example, how many people love their jobs? How many people are happy and fulfilled? *Just walk around – many people are miserable and negative. They have a lot of problems, but do not have solutions.* They are victims of their own self-imposed or societal-imposed limitations, which is what I call bullshit. Much of what we are fed is bullshit to a greater or lesser degree, so we learn to lessen ourselves and everyone around us. My job is to empower people, lift them, light a fire within them, show them their own greatness, change their thoughts and emotions, making them come alive and feel powerful. That is my job. That is what I was born to do, and I am wholeheartedly doing it.

You were not put on this earth to work and die.
You were not put on this earth to suffer.
You were not put on this earth to pop out a bunch of babies.
You were not put on this earth to serve everyone else at the expense of yourself.

You were put on this earth to use your ***personal power*** influencing change and transformation, making the world a better place for all of us. You have a mission and a purpose, a life purpose. **You have been massively lied to.**

The 7 Types of Power

There are seven known and distinguished types of power. *They are as follows: Legitimate Power, Coercive Power, Expert Power, Informational Power, Reward Power, Connection Power, and Referent Power.*

Legitimate Power – when someone is in a position of power. Such as our US President.

Coercive Power – having power using control, manipulation, or coercion. Coercive power is unwarranted.

Expert Power – power you have from being an expert in something. A good example is your education or credentials.

Informational Power – power that comes from knowing or having certain information and being knowledgeable about a subject.

Reward Power – having power by administering awards, praises, validation, recognition, promotions, and other rewards, both intrinsic and extrinsic.

Connection Power – networking power or being connected to people while gaining favor and being a positive resource for them.

Referent Power – power by building and developing relationships.

Self-Efficacy

Self-efficacy is an individual's innate belief in their own ability to complete a task or achieve a goal. It is the confident embodiment of total belief and faith to create or influence their environment and circumstances. You are the **CREATOR** in your life. Some people know and embrace this, and some people don't. ***Successful/productive people embrace their self-efficacy, while helpless/dependent people do not.*** In psychology, this is known as your ***Locus of Control.*** You either have an ***Internal Locus of Control or an External Locus of Control.*** In my own words and definitions, the ***Locus of Control*** can be defined in terms of the ***productive*** and the ***unproductive*** or the ***helpful*** and the ***helpless.***

Individuals with an ***Internal Locus of Control*** are responsible, productive, and helpful; they are the **CREATORS** of their own realities and destinies. On the other hand, individuals with an ***External Locus of Control*** are usually unproductive and helpless. They have a fierce, unwavering belief that the world and other people owe them something. ***External Locus of Control*** people tend to be ***extremely entitled.*** They feel they are owed everything; therefore, they do absolutely nothing. ***They wait for things to fall into their laps.*** One of my clients has a daughter with an ***External Locus of Control*** who is selfishly entitled; she believes the world owes her everything. ***For example, she has never gotten her own job.*** In every job she has ever had, someone else got it for her or recommended it to her.

She has never taken responsibility applying for and seeking out her own employment. In the same fashion, she has never gotten her own boyfriend. She expects that everyone else will introduce her playing matchmaker. ***SHE TAKES NO ACTION BUT EXPECTS OTHERS TO TAKE ALL THE ACTION FOR HER.*** She never did her own homework; her mother did her homework for her. She expects to be handheld and spoon-fed – must be nice! ***The problem with the entitled members of society is that everyone around them enables them.*** Everyone around the entitled sees the entitled as helpless ***(because the entitled acts helpless)***; therefore, the enabling is perpetuated.

The world is divided evenly between givers and takers. In these examples, the entitled **External Locus of Control** people are takers and everyone around them is a giver, endlessly giving to them. This creates inequity. ***Personally, I would love it if someone kissed and wiped my ass every day, but because I am a CREATOR, I am not entitled or enabled because I have an Internal Locus of Control.***

Your ass is either being wiped by someone else (taker), or it is you who is doing the wiping of asses (giver).

This is unjust. Everyone should be a **CREATOR**. Everyone is a **CREATOR**. ***But if you don't see yourself as a CREATOR and you don't take momentous action, you will be unsuccessful.***

<u>Successful people take momentous ACTION.</u> They do not complain or whine. They do not act entitled. They don't expect ass-wiping or handholding. ***They are usually underprivileged and come from nothing at all. They are hungry, so they act, move, and create. Through that CREATION, they become massively successful.*** They embody an **Internal Locus of Control.**

The takers are not successful. They do not act; they only take from others. They complain, whine, and gripe often. ***Everyone else is responsible for their happiness and emotional stability.*** Everyone must bow down and serve them. This is why 30- and 40-year-olds still live with mommy not working or contributing to the household in any way (they are being enabled).

Creators have **self-efficacy.** The entitled do not because they are entitled. **Entitled people do not believe in themselves; they only believe that other people will bow down and worship them and kiss their ass.**

Many grown adults in marriages and relationships can be categorized as Peter Pan and Wendy. Peter Pan never grows up (entitled, taker, enabled). Wendy is the responsible one. **She is the giver and the enabler.**

Psychological Capital

Psychological Capital is the psychological or mental resources that help an individual live a fulfilled and productive life. **The four components of PsyCap are 1) Hope- the ability to achieve goals and create the future 2) Efficacy- the belief in one's own abilities 3) Resilience- the ability to bounce back moving on from hurtful or harmful events 4) Optimism- a positive outlook on outcomes.**

In other words, **Psychological Capital** means we are born with all the resources inside of ourselves **right now** to be massively productive and successful. People think tangible resources are the keys to success, but they are not. Things like money, mentors, property, and material goods can and will certainly aid in your success journey, but they don't really matter that much. **However, intangible resources such as knowledge, intuition, determination, tenacity, emotion, problem-solving, creativity, intelligence, and human relations skills are what will ultimately drive a person to massive success, fame, and fortune.**

What this means is that you were already born with these special gifts (intangible resources) that will guide you and make you ridiculously successful. I come from nothing. Growing up, we were an average middle-class family. I became successful by using my internal **(Psychological Capital)** or (intangible resources) achieving massive success in my career.

Goal Setting

Think about what you really want. Manifestation is an **EMBODIMENT, *and you will wholeheartedly attract WHAT YOU ARE***. Identify those things you really want for yourself. Your dreams. Your ambitions. **Your 'why'.** Goal Setting is an action plan broken down into simplistic and smaller tasks. All goals require **EMPOWERED ACTION.** You must move to achieve anything; you must take *empowered action.*

STEP 1: Identify the big goal.

STEP 2: Identify smaller sub-goals.

STEP 3: Identify the **EMPOWERED ACTIONS** you will take.

STEP 4: Take action and make no excuses.

STEP 5: Notice how things begin unfolding for you. ***Things begin to make themselves available to you.***

You should have:

- ➢ Daily goals
- ➢ Weekly goals
- ➢ Monthly goals
- ➢ Quarterly goals
- ➢ Yearly goals
- ➢ Decade goals
- ➢ Lifetime goals

You can chunk any goal down into bite-size tasks making accomplishing your goal much easier. Some goals seem too big to accomplish, but that is simply not true if you chunk them down. Focus more on daily, weekly, and monthly goals. Remember the ***Law of Motion. Newton's First Law of Motion is the Law of Inertia, which states that an object at rest will remain at rest, and an object in motion will remain in motion unless acted upon by an external force.***

How does this apply to you?

Many people sit in *inertia* unable to move or act. You might call them lazy and/or unmotivated, but if they don't take action and don't *go into motion,* they will remain at rest, never having accomplished what they want to accomplish. Similarly, an object in motion will stay in motion because it has gained **MOMENTUM.** You need **MOMENTUM.** Accomplishing these smaller daily and weekly goals will give you **MOMENTUM** so that you will remain in motion. Keep moving forward no matter what. *Let no other person or situation obstruct your mission.* In *The Concise Mastery*, Robert Greene asserts, "In moving toward mastery, you are bringing your mind closer to reality and to life itself. Anything that is alive is in a continual state of change and movement. The moment that you rest, thinking that you have attained the level you desire, a part of your mind enters a phase of decay. You lose your hard-earned creativity, and others begin to sense it. This is a power and intelligence that must be continually renewed, or it will die."

Vision

You are a *visionary.* You can see the *bigger picture.* Everything you've ever thought can come true. Your subconscious mind cannot understand the difference between reality and imagination. What is thought in the mind is actualized in reality. *It is okay to dream.* I spend most of my time dreaming because I hate the drudgery of reality. *I get lost in my ideas, goals, and dreams, and you should too.* Napoleon Hill, in *Success Through a Positive Mental Attitude,* says this about the subconscious mind, "In effect, the subconscious mind is like a battery. From it, you can obtain tremendous surges of mental and spiritual energy, which often transmute into physical vitality. These jolts of energy will go to waste if we permit them to be short-circuited by needless negative emotions. But used constructively, this energy can multiply itself many times, just as a powerhouse generator produces vast amounts of useful power."

Start by setting small daily and weekly goals. Take time building momentum and motivation. Everything has a process and timing is crucial. **Things do not happen overnight, but they do happen and will happen for you.** Commit yourself to a better life. Commit to giving yourself all the desires of your heart.

Discover Your Potential

Do you know your potential? Search deep within your innermost being asking yourself these questions.

1. Who am I?
2. What do I need?
3. What do I want?
4. What do I like?
5. What inspires me?
6. What gives me joy?
7. What makes me feel fulfilled?
8. Why do I exist?
9. What is my purpose?
10. What is my intention?
11. What are my skills?
12. What are my talents?
13. What stops me?
14. What makes me feel small?
15. How can I remove my blockages?

Potential is something we are all born with. **Potential is the capacity to become or develop into something or someone.** It means making manifest your desires. We all feel so limited, but we are not. **Our limitations are only psychological, which means we made them up. They are not real. It is time to accept and embrace how brilliant and creative you are.**

Spend a lot of time in **deep reflection**, asking yourself over and over – **What is my highest potential? What can I become?**

There are only two things that stop you. They are:

1. Fear
2. Doubt

Both *fear and doubt* are CRIPPLING. Let me give you an illustration. I was afraid to release my first book, **GIRL GRIT: SAVAGE NOT AVERAGE** because I was afraid of what people might think of it. ***As a first-time author, that thought scared me.*** **GIRL GRIT: SAVAGE NOT AVERAGE** is authentic and parts of it are vulnerable. I take a **bullshit-free approach** giving my readers an honest account of some of the harsher challenges of reality. It's a book that will either deeply resonate with you, and you will love it, or you might be offended by some of the content. ***Being offended just means you are being challenged (which is not a bad thing).***

Being a girl isn't really a pleasant experience. We face many challenges around being controlled, feeling less than others, rape and sexual assault, failed relationships, mental health issues, pregnancy and postpartum, single motherhood, gender roles and domestic responsibilities, difficulties and discrimination in professional life, harassment, etc. ***If you have not experienced any of these things, consider yourself very blessed because it is many people's reality.***

I got over my fears and doubts because they were crippling me. I wrote **GIRL GRIT: SAVAGE NOT AVERAGE** because the message needed to get out. Women need to hear it. I noticed **universal suffering** with my own eyes. I wanted to do something about it. I wanted to solve the problem, so I wrote **GIRL GRIT: SAVAGE NOT AVERAGE,** my first book. Leading up to the release, I had so many fears such as, ***"What are people going to think?" But the truth is, it doesn't matter what people think or whether they like the book. It serves a specific purpose for a specific audience. That is all that matters at the end of the day.***

Authenticity and Vulnerability

Authenticity and vulnerability are POWERFUL when it comes to building relationships. I am incredibly authentic and vulnerable with my readers *because I am building trust and rapport with them through my writing.* When we are open and honest, we break the ice. We gain buy-in and trust from others, making it easier for us to persuade, help, and build relationships. This is the truth. This is the message readers need to hear. The world is fake, but people don't like fake. They like real, honest, and authentic. People are knowledge-seekers. There is only knowledge in the truth, not fakeness or facades.

People are afraid to be authentic and vulnerable because of guilt and shame, but again, guilt and shame only live in your head (just like fear) – they don't really exist. They are ghosts that follow you around holding you back from reaching your full potential. ***Fear, shame, doubt, and guilt all keep you from being great.***

The Great Distraction

Our lives are what I call **The Great Distraction** because most people are not doing what they REALLY want to do. Many people are scraping by, trying to keep their head screwed on straight as best as possible. Many people are negative, sad, angry, and depressed at best. Just go outside and look around you. Many people work jobs they don't want to be at, their kids don't listen, their partner is cheating on them making their life hell, they lack confidence and self-esteem, they have bad and unhealthy habits that create poor health, they have little time for anything enjoyable, many live paycheck to paycheck, they listen to the negative people in their lives, they constantly self-sabotage, they wonder why all of their childhood dreams died and to add insult to injury they may have unresolved and unhealed trauma from childhood.

Everything, in essence, becomes a distraction, including but not limited to your kids, spouse, their school bullshit, their activities, TV, social media, your parents and family, friends, the news, notifications, pop-ups, advertisements, traffic, rude people, manipulators, your mental health, food, alcohol, substances, etc. *A distraction is anything that takes you away from what really matters.* I am not saying your kids, spouse, and family do not matter. I am saying that the excessive concern and involvement in their lives and well-being does. *It is easy to get taken from an important task you are focusing on to a less important task.* One example is when I am writing, and someone calls or texts me intercepting my flow.

I call this *The Great Distraction* because life gets busy. Who would you be right now if reality never set in? This means that if you never got married, had kids, or were working a job you hated, *what else would you be doing right now? Would you experience more fulfillment and a higher quality of life?* Life itself is *The Great Distraction*. Another example is my daughter's school, which completely takes over my life. The school sends numerous emails and notifications per week, every week, like 3-4 things that are going on that you must volunteer for, take off work for, remember to bring in, buy or do.

I feel that the parent becomes more of the student than the actual student. This school acts like no one works, and we can just come in for this and that all the time whenever asked. I have learned to ignore 80% of it because it was driving me crazy. I had to learn that my daughter's K-12 education doesn't matter. Yes, it matters in the sense that it is her foundational education, but at the end of the day, it is a K-12 education. Although your K-12 education is important, it is meaningless in the actual workforce and is not a determinant of success. Just look at my K-12 report card, and you will notice more Cs and Ds compared to As and Bs.

Learn to omit meaningless distractions, focusing on more important tasks and goals. **You will get bogged down by the bullshit.** Identify what matters and what doesn't remove all that which does not produce or add value to your life. <u>**It is impossible to step on a woman who is always flying.**</u>

Things Every Person Wants

Every person comes into this world virtually the same on a blank slate. Yes, we are born into different families, circumstances, and geographical areas, but every human being is born a human being, no matter your assigned birth sex. Your brain is a blank slate that has not been put through any mental filters, conditioning, or experiences of any kind. We are all more similar than we are different. **_The differences come from:_**

> ➢ Teachings/Programming/Conditioning
> ➢ Social Environment
> ➢ Behavioral Influences and Learning
> ➢ Situations and Circumstances
> ➢ Experiences
> ➢ Trauma
> ➢ Culture and Geographical Locations
> ➢ Who raised you and their dispositions
> ➢ Education, Values, and Beliefs of your parents
> ➢ Religious and Political Influences and Beliefs

These influences make us different and shape our personalities, values, beliefs, maps of the world affecting how we perceive, understand, relate, and associate in different social situations. **_Fundamentally, as human beings, we are all the same._** _There are certain things every single person wants. Here they are:_

> ➢ We all want to be loved.
> ➢ We all want to feel important and feel like we matter.
> ➢ We all want to do something important bringing value to the world through our talents and creativity.
> ➢ We all want to be liked and accepted by others.

- ➤ We want to be appreciated and recognized.
- ➤ We want to belong and feel included.
- ➤ We have pure hearts filled with good intentions.
- ➤ We never mean actual harm to anyone.
- ➤ We all want to be good people bringing goodness to the world.
- ➤ We all want to be seen, heard, listened to, and validated.
- ➤ We all want to bless and serve others.
- ➤ We all want to help others.
- ➤ We all want to give back being generous with our time and resources.
- ➤ We all want to love hard.

You might be asking, but what are the bad people? What about the Narcissists and manipulators, the self-centered, the unprincipled, the criminals, the haters, and the morally depreciated?

Understand that their situations, circumstances, environment, and social programming made them that way. ***There is no such thing as a bad person, only unwanted behaviors.*** **Don't you suppose that every person sitting in prison right now wasn't once brutalized as a small and innocent child who couldn't have a voice for themselves?**

Many people suffer from things they cannot talk about.

We all desire goodness, wholeness, love, prosperity, abundance, joy, peace, and kindness. You have no idea how much your upbringing and social environments impact and influence every single area of your life. Most people do not think their childhood influences them so much as an adult, but it does. It really does. If you are f*cked up, as so many of us unfortunately are, you can do something about it. **You can unf*ck yourself. You can grow, evolve, improve, ascend, do better, be better, read more, learn more, help yourself, receive love and support from others. I grow and improve every day in every way.**

Sister – You possess an abundance of power and influence.

Chapter 3 Takeaways

- ➤ Power is only discovered within and does not come from external sources.
- ➤ Boxes of power lie unopened inside of you.
- ➤ There are **seven known types of Power**
- ➤ **Self-efficacy** is the belief in your ability to act and create.
- ➤ Leverage your **Psychological Capital** impacting your power and influence.
- ➤ Establish clear, direct, focused, and achievable goals.
- ➤ Use vision to see into the future. **Activate your Third Eye.**
- ➤ Life is **The Great Distraction.** Do not let it derail you, your progress, and your success.

Share Your Story:

In the space provided, it is time to share your story. What types of power do you possess? How can you leverage more power in your life?

Chapter 4
Fantasies

*"And the professor kept asking me why I wanted my PhD. I did not know what to say; I just wanted it. But deep down, I knew. I knew because I did not want to f*cking suffer anymore. I wanted to wake up."*

"Everything has beauty, but not everyone sees it" – Confucius.

The Chase

Ahh, the thrill of the chase. This is a phenomenon I have wrestled with for a long time, and I am about to expand my perspective on it. ***The thrill of the chase simply means we want what we cannot have.*** It is when we do not have something (and not when we have it) that that item or person becomes ***more valuable*** in our eyes. We begin romanticizing and idealizing that person or object of our deepest desires. ***You can only desire something or someone when it does not belong to you.*** This is the problem with love and why people constantly fall in and out of love as often as they go to the restroom. ***Love is triggered by feelings, and feelings fluctuate depending on what is going on in the immediate environment.***

We place more value on something or someone we do not have; that is just Psychology 101. All psychology is ***reverse psychology,*** which is why they say the definition of insanity is doing the same thing over and over while expecting different results. ***By using reverse psychology in all situations, you can effortlessly get exactly what you want; you must understand how the human mind works and how powerful an emotion like desire is.***

The truth is, we are all chasing something. It could be a person, a feeling, an object, or a situation/opportunity. We all chase. We are good at chasing, but we are not good at attracting. ***Learn*** *how to stop chasing and start attracting.* We are chasing things and people that we will never catch because those things and or people are **not available** to be caught. I will provide a good example of this below. *We chase when something is missing inside of ourselves... there is something we lack, a hole inside that must be filled with the object or person of our desire.*

Edgy – The Super Bad Boy

I have fallen in love with Satan repeatedly. If he proposed to me, I would say yes. We are fiercely attracted to bad boys. We get bored of the good and excited by the bad. *The bad are much more enigmatic and elusive.*

I am wildly attracted to bad boys. Why? *Because I want what I cannot have.* Satan does a great job of teasing us. *He shows us what we want but never actually gives himself to us.* We end up chasing him forever. Chasing the bad boy. Bad boys do not give themselves away so easily. *They are puzzling, elusive, and mysterious – masters of the game, masters at playing hard to get. They are not open to anyone.* They have a hidden inner world filled with deep, dark secrets about their past. *Their love is a prized possession because it is so rare and fleeting, which is precisely what makes a bad boy so annoyingly attractive to me.* Or so my old unhealed ass felt.

I met a man I call Edgy on a dating app. I named him Edgy because he has a very Edgy look and demeanor. He even had a 666 filter on the top of his forehead in one photo – doomed for trouble. I found him attractive, but I was afraid to message him after matching. **<u>Something was eerie about this man but in a very sexy, almost dangerous way.</u>** He had a very dark, stern, and masculine look with a face that looked like he wanted to kill someone. I sent him a message, and he replied. I looked at his photos again feeling apprehensive. *I do not know what it was about him.* He was soulless and mysterious. He sucked me in; I was intrigued. *He had deep eyes wider than an ocean with a look that could pierce your soul consuming your mind with thoughts* *of obsession, tension, and sexual desire.* I vacillated for days as to whether I should respond to him, but I eventually did so five days later.

He responded again, and then we started talking regularly. He is sweet and kind, contrary to his looks, but still, I can't fully trust him. Yes, I suppose I am judging a book by its cover at this stage. Edgy is not who I would consider to be a bad boy, but rather, a **Super Bad Boy,** and that made him all the sexier and *more mysterious. A Super Bad Boy is a rare bad boy, the King of Bad Boys. King Bad Boy. A Super Bad Boy makes Bad Boys look like a saint.*

Edgy drove me wild. The first question he asked me was, "are you a sexual person?" FLASH, FLASH, FLASH, RED FLAG ALERT! Last I checked, I have a pulse, so yes, I am a sexual person. **We are sexual beings, after all, and we are created to have sexual experiences – that is just human nature.** When I first met Edgy, I knew this was going to be strictly a hook-up situation since he came on strong about sex. But, after a week of talking, I fell head over heels in love with him craving him deeply, passionately, and intimately. He is the kind of guy I wanted to burn the kitchen down with. I met him just before the 4th of July, and I can confidently say the sparks were flying hard and fast.

I loved Edgy because he was the ultimate challenge. He gave me a chase. He was not easy, and he did not throw himself at me. Nothing is more unattractive than when someone throws themselves at you. *Edgy made me feel deeply.* This is very powerful - *<u>when you can make someone feel, you can make them do almost anything because you must remember that everyone wants to feel.</u> This is why when guys lose the "spark" for you or fall out of love, it is game over, and they dump you. To make a guy feel for you and to keep the spark going long-term, you must remain <u>detached and elusive.</u>* Inflict pain, suspense, and unpredictability. **No one wants boring and predictable.** This is why the **No Contact Rule** is one of the biggest rules in dating; there is no greater way to inflict pain than No Contact. *Ignoring someone is the deepest type of pain there is. <u>Emotional neglect is a direct childhood wound for many of us.</u>*

The Mother

Many men did not have emotionally available mothers. This is why the woman who makes herself emotionally available to a man, he will get bored and leave her. Playing men do not appreciate women being nice, loyal, and loving – *they want the <u>emotionally unavailable</u> <u>woman who resembles their mother so they can possess her.</u>* It gives him the chase or the challenge he needs. He could not win Mommy's love, and her love was oh-so-valuable. *Make your love valuable and disappear.* Your love should be rare and not freely given; make him work hard for it.

Similarly, we women respond to the emotionally unavailable man because there is nothing, we want more than to be visible to our fathers, to have daddy's love. Emotional unavailability, aka indifference, is more than sexy…it drives us crazy. Being mindful of your **emotional world** is the first big step in understanding attachment and emotions. The anxiety or butterflies or sparks you feel are just emotions, nothing more and nothing less. The reason you feel anxiety, or an **activated attachment system** is because, deep down, you are going after someone or something that is **unattainable**. You love a man who will never belong to you. **You covet him and his rare love.** But you cannot have him… and this is why they advise us to play games in dating… boring leads to uninterested and uninterested leads to break up. **Everyone wants to feel; remember that. Love is not love; love is pain.**

The Power of the Fairytale / Fantasy

For most people, life is simply boring. It is routine. It is common and it is familiar. Yes, we do things that bring joy, purpose, and happiness, but most of our everyday lives are boring.

Understand that there is extreme power and influence in the Fairytale or Fantasy. Most people idealize and romanticize everything and everyone. We all have these ideas or constructions in our mind about what a certain person is really like or not like. However, those ideas or constructions are not real; they are simply how we perceive that person and not who that other person is.

We get swept into fairytales and fantasies because they promise something better, something that will rescue us from the mundane or pain and suffering in our lives. We all believe in fairytales and fantasies to a greater or lesser degree. This is why the concept of marriage is extremely dangerous and harmful for a lot of people. **When most people think of marriage, they think of marriage on the frontend and not the backend.** They think of the beginning stages of marriage, such as the wedding, the ceremony, the parties, the honeymoon, and possibly the first couple of years. They are not thinking about the long-term, 5+ years into the marriage, the bills, the changes, the emotions, the disagreements, the problems, the weight gain, and issues that arise. They think of marriage in terms of hope or the promise of the fairytale/fantasy side or idealization/romanticized version of marriage.

Marriage is not cracked up to be what the media makes it out to be. In this sense, fantasies and fairytales are dangerous. They can serve as traps. This is not to negate good marriages or to surmise that all marriages are doomed, but with the divorce rate being astronomical, my point stands. Yes, you will have good, healthy life-giving marriages, but right now, I am speaking about the shit marriages— *the relationshits.* In marriages where the woman becomes a *glutton for punishment* and not the princess, she sees herself as growing up. *Self-sacrificing at the expense of self-esteem is never the right choice.*

There is another side to fantasies and fairytales. You can use them to your advantage. Promise someone a fantasy or fairytale, and you can get them to do whatever you want them to do – *I mean, isn't this what men have been doing to women for centuries? FUTURE FAKING!* Promising them happily ever after to get services from them and then turning around and treating them like shit while annihilating their self-esteems? *I am telling you ladies, always always dish out to them what they dish out to you.* Take back your power, being mean gives you that opportunity. No one likes a *glutton for punishment*, yet women do it all the time. They constantly bow down and worship the man who walks all over them. This is called walking on eggshells. *Cowering is not attractive but standing tall and firm is. The sexiest characteristic of any person is confidence. Confidence is strength and strength is power. And with power, the ball will always be in your court.*

Promise them a fairytale, but do not deliver it. Keep them chasing, keep them wanting more.

Sketchy

I gave Edgy the heebie-jeebies because he called me one day drunk and asked me if I "f*cked him off?" Which didn't make sense to me, but he meant that he scared me away. We had not met yet, and I was playing hard to get keeping my value high. He took my distance and elusiveness as "f*cking him off," or more precisely, "to f*ck off," is how most people would put it. I told him, "No, you did not f*ck me off." He told me to come over, so I went. I was in love with him. It took me 45 minutes to get ready, and then I was driving in my car to see my Edgy. I was so excited driving to his house; it took me about an hour to get there. I was so nervous and excited; I had the heebie-jeebies too. In fact, my friends started calling him the Heebie-Jeebies guy because I would jump through the roof whenever he texted me. His texts gave me a *sudden high.* I loved getting attention from this guy.

When I got to Sketchy's house, I mean Edgy, it was sketchy. I renamed Edgy Sketchy. His house was falling apart, but I guessed it worked for him. For example, his toilet didn't flush, and he never bothered fixing it. I asked him how he managed to take shits. He told me that he only shits at work. Okay then, problem solved, I suppose – don't fix your toilet. When I had to pee, I had to throw my toilet paper into the waste basket (thank God he at least had a waste basket in the bathroom!) I made sure not to eat much so that I didn't have to shit at his house…

Sketchy was excited that I was there. He's a fun and cool guy. A drunk bad boy with an edge to him. He is my age. We had good conversations. He told me I was the kind of person he wanted to eat trash pizza and watch old movies with. It was sweet. Because we are both into music, we played music trivia, and it was so intense because we were tied up until the very end. I completely dominated him with the last few songs. Because it was 80s music trivia, the song *Heartbreak Beat* by the Psychedelic Furs came on, and he sang/serenaded that song to me, and it was sweetly romantic. Sketchy can sing. That was another HUGE turn-on for me. A man can make me melt with music, literally. Music is my life.

I had a great time with Sketchy. It felt like we were two teenagers back in the 90s, just being silly and enjoying life. He was so wasted though falling over many times. I had to keep picking him up and dusting him off. I could tell this might become a co-dependent relationship with me being the rescuer, so I decided that Sketchy and I wouldn't make it long-term.

Sketchy was all fun and games and nothing more – no depth, unfortunately, not when you drink incessantly. But I did have a great time with him. ***I got to be a teenager again for 12 hours; what is that worth?*** I got to forget life and all my problems. I got to pee in a toilet that didn't flush. ***All of life is nothing more than an experience. And each experience is a gift.***

Looking back on all this now, I smile and laugh at the same time. I will never forget Edgy. He served a purpose in my life, even if only for one night. *Edgy was a good reminder that life IS SUPPOSED TO BE LIGHT AND FUN.* You aren't supposed to take everything so seriously all the time. We are meant to live, to explore, to experience, and to have GOOD TIMES. Edgy is a Let the Good Times Roll kind of guy. That's what makes him so special and memorable. *I only have fond memories when I think of Edgy, even if I did have to piss in a broken toilet for the night.*

What Village?

When a woman gets pregnant, she has these ideas in her head about having a village because she has heard it said a thousand times that it takes a village to raise a child. Yes, it takes a village to raise a child. This is a fact. She has ideas that if she brings a child into the world, she will have this village that she has been promised by society because of that old adage. *But my question is, what village?* Where is this village we all speak of? Women either have a village, or they do not. And many do not. No one is chomping at the bit offering love and support on your mothering journey.

Some women DO have a village. This is not to argue that none of us have villages. I am arguing that many of us do not. Sometimes, not even our own husband or partner is a village. Sometimes, your male partner/spouse could be living in another village, county, state, or country as far as you know. *Women want to believe at conception that there is help and support.*

No woman signs up to do this shit alone and sad. No woman signs up to be a single mom, ever! I am not speaking to those women who have villages but rather those who do not. I have always been fiercely independent, not because I wanted to be but because I had to be. No one ever wants to be alone. No one ever wants to maneuver through life with no help, support, or assistance, but some of us are left with no choice.

No one is stepping up to volunteer or lend a hand. There is no sympathy, no empathy, and no care. It is just you and your grit. I argue that many of you feel alone, sad, and unsupported in your motherhood journey, which makes motherhood harder on you when you feel so isolated. *Motherhood is so hard.*

You still must be a mother when...

1. You are sick.
2. You are tired.
3. You are angry or sad.
4. When someone hurts you.
5. When someone abandons you.
6. When someone cheats on you.
7. When you have had no break.
8. When you are at work.
9. When you are on a business trip.
10. Even when you are on your death bed.

There is no break and no end in sight. It is a never-ending exhausting existence. Many of us are even pushed into motherhood, especially if we grew up in a Christian or religious home like I did, because motherhood, after all, is the acme of your existence as you know it. We are shamed and blamed if we get pregnant too young, too early, or out of wedlock. We get shamed and blamed if we do not marry or have children by a certain age before it is too late, and the clock is done ticking. We rush and race into motherhood when many of us are not healed enough to be a parent in the first place. *You need to be really f*cking healed and really f*cking patient to be an effective, resourceful, and kind parent.*

All motherhood is work. I do not hate motherhood; I am discussing a very real reality that we all experience every day, those of us who are mothers. Yes, we love our kids. Yes, they are our world. Yes, we would do anything for them. Yes, they bring us joy. But we would be f*cking lying if we did not express how hard motherhood is. *When you fall apart, you must still be* *a mother.* I remember, after my divorce, I felt vulnerable, unloved, and desperate. I remember my daughter was holding me in my bed late at night. I lay there crying because I had NO ONE to hold onto. That is when I realized that my life required me to be far stronger than I ever signed up for; to be far stronger than I ever wanted or thought I could be.

Acknowledge the truth and acknowledge how you really feel. I never signed up to be a single mom. I do not even understand how I am making it, but I am somehow making it. Because I felt like I was NOTHING my entire life, I thought motherhood would make me something, that it would make me whole, but it has not. That is a lie from society.

How can you get help when you have no help? For me, I must pay for most of the help I get except for family *very occasionally* stepping in. I knew I needed to make a lot of money so I could hire the help I needed. I also prayed a lot and asked my guides for help and support. They did provide help and support in subtle ways.

Sometimes, there is no village; sometimes, it is just you and your grit.

Give Me a Break!

Every day, I pray for miracles. I pray for breaks or my next big breakthrough. One Thursday afternoon, on a day like any other day, I received a rather unusual email, exactly one month after the international release of **GIRL GRIT: SAVAGE NOT AVERAGE,** from a representative from a well-known Hollywood film company (I will not mention the name protecting the film company). The subject of the email, *Book Approved for Film Adaptation.* Here is the email I was sent verbatim:

Dear Dr. Alexandra Elinsky,

I trust this email finds you in good health and high spirits.

We are delighted to reach out to you regarding your book, **"GIRL GRIT."** After a meticulous evaluation, we are thrilled to inform you that your book has been selected as one of the exclusive Content Titles for adaptation into a film. We have entered into a collaboration with **Netflix**, and we are honored to extend a contract to you, offering to acquire film rights as one of our distinguished pioneering projects.

Our accomplished team has already allocated the estimated budget for the film's production, and we have assembled a skilled production team to bring your vision to life. Prior to commencing the project, **Name of Film Company Films** will have an exclusive contract with you as the esteemed author. It is crucial to maintain strict confidentiality regarding all project-related information, and we shall include a comprehensive non-disclosure clause within the contract. The film's release date will be announced by the production company in due course.

As the authorized representative of the rights holder, and with **Name of Film Company Films** as the acquiring entity, you will be responsible for processing all necessary licenses, permits, registrations, and document signings exclusively with us to facilitate the transfer. We will furnish you with a separate contract between yourself and **Name of Film Company Films**, and we will promptly forward the film agreement documentation for your review and confirmation.

We kindly request your timely response, as we eagerly anticipate the opportunity to collaborate with you on this remarkable endeavor.

Please provide the best phone number at which to reach you.

Thank you for considering our offer, and we look forward to the pleasure of working together.

Warmest regards,

I was instantly frozen; can it be so? Do they want to acquire the rights to adapt **GIRL GRIT** into a film? Unbelievable! I replied enthusiastically, stating my interest; within an hour, this representative, calling himself Henry, sent me a very convincing, detailed, and impressive contract, offer, and non-disclosure agreement. The contract was 11 pages, delineating his offer of $550,000 to me, the budget for the film was $3.1M, and production dates for both pre-and-postproduction. Nothing in the contract and non-disclosure seemed in any way off to me. It all looked and felt legitimate. I was freaking out! Can this be real?

Henry set up a time to call me on the phone to discuss the details of his offer to acquire the film rights. When he called, everything sounded legit except for one part: they didn't have a screenplay! He asked if I had one, and of course, I didn't; I had only authored the book. He said no worries and that he would reach out to the WGA (Writer's Guild of America) to solicit a screenwriter for my book. Twenty-four hours later, he called back and said he had found a screenwriter for **GIRL GRIT**, but I had to front $8,000 (a discounted price because it would normally cost $20,000) to have this writer produce the screenplay. At this point, I knew it was a scam, but I played dumb to see how far the rabbit trail led. Henry sent me a contract for the screenplay and an invoice for $8,000.

Unlike the first contract, the screenplay contract was a joke. It was vague asf. The invoice was also a joke; this company called Fake Ass Bullshit LLC (protecting the real company name) was a legitimate LLC registered eight months before I received this fake offer. This famous Hollywood production company didn't invoice me. Fake Ass Bullshit LLC did. FAB LLC also had a fake website that was laughable at best and atrocious at worst. There was hardly any information on this website. Upon further investigation, Henry had me wiring the $8,000 to a 30-year-old woman in Arizona. I instantly found her on Google and LinkedIn since she did not have a common name. Easily traceable. She looked normal and innocent (insert laughing emoji) and operated another business in a completely different industry. Google gave me plenty of information about her and FAB LLC. She is a registered member of FAB LLC, which is her FAB business. Her mailing address was a PO Box. She had several PO Boxs affiliated with her name (sketchy).

As elaborate as this scam was, trust me when I say that if there is a Top Scammers of the Year award, it would go to FAB LLC and this young woman. Who in their right mind would think anyone is stupid enough to fall for this as good as they made it sound? Yes, the offer was impressively enticing, but firstly, you are offering to pay me $550,000 for the rights to MY BOOK and then proceed to ask me for a measly $8,000 (in comparison) to $550,000 for just the screenplay. You have got to be out of your mind.

When he sent me the invoice and screenplay contract, I replied to Henry and said, take the $8,000 cost of the screenplay out of your $3.1M budget. He then asked me to call again, and I just ignored everything. End of story. This is what you call thievery. These morons are THIEVES! Try and steal from a single mother. They are full of shit. The worst part might be how much these idiots rattled my emotions. I am not someone who gets rattled easily as I pride myself on my insane levels of emotional control and mastery; however, when you are promising me $550,000 plus 2-3% of revenue share to turn MY BOOK (MY BABY) into a movie, how can I not get excited about the possibility of that happening for me? Not only were they trying to get $8,000 out of me fast, but they also put me into an emotional whirlwind by f*cking with my emotions. First, I was very excited and happy just to be massively let down. Thank God, I didn't give them any money, but still. I emailed the production company they were pretending to be helping protect them and their reputation. I also reported FAB LLC to the Federal Trade Commission.

Given the fact that I had her name, PO Box, business name, bank information, and contact info (say I had sent her $8,000) and then realized it was a scam after the fact, didn't her dumb ass think I could sue the shit out of her for scamming me? **How do people honestly think they can get away with this stuff?**

What's the Point?

The point is, in all business transactions, both legitimate and scams, you must be very careful. Anytime you are given a contract, always have a qualified attorney review it. Do not give anyone money online that you have just met (no matter how enticing their offer seems). Always do your **due diligence. Research both the company and the individual.** Any emails should ALWAYS come from a company email account and not Gmail, Hotmail, Yahoo, or the like. Scrutinize them, ask questions, and always look at **past customer reviews.** Take your time, and **do not make hasty financial decisions because it sounds good.** Beware of **quick actions.** Often, marketers and advertisers try to get you to **act now** or **act fast** by offering deals that **expire quickly** or by **putting unnecessary time constraints on things. Do not listen to those.** It is all a **marketing tactic** used to get your money **NOW.** Always be careful and never act fast. Yes, they want your money NOW but trust me when I say, they will be just as happy to take it in 30 days from now once you've done your **due diligence** on them. **No offer is ever expiring, and you will NOT miss out.** This is called the **Law of Scarcity**, playing on people's **FOMO (Fear of Missing Out),** making you believe you will miss out on a great offer if you don't act now. It is all bullshit just to get your money as quickly and painlessly as possible.

Scams are all around us. Since we live in a technologically advanced age where everything is online, it is easy for scammers to hide behind fake companies, made-up names pretending to be someone they are not. **We are all susceptible to manipulation and schemes,** especially when they sound good and influence our emotions. Do not take the bait. This can also happen in jobs. For example, you are hired to be a Research Assistant because you are great at research, and on your first day of work, your new employer tells you you will not be doing research anymore. You will be doing accounting. You have no idea how to do accounting because you have never done it before. ***This is why job descriptions are so important.***

This happened to me when I was 28 years old and still in my doctoral program. I found this small boutique company online, hiring an **Organizational Development Consultant.** I applied and went through three rounds of interviews. For the third interview, I had to fly across the country (I lived on the east side and they the west) for an in-person interview (half-day interview), where I planned and delivered a 4-hour facilitation session for their entire team. The role was heavily coaching and training, which is my specialty (literally what I got my doctorate in). I spent weeks planning the perfect 4-hour training session, selecting and preparing the best content for their team of 10 individuals. Of course, I did exceedingly well and was offered the position of **Organizational Development Consultant** that same day! They offered me 90K for the position. For a 28-year-old, that offer was not bad at all and realistic for the role. I paid for this trip; they did not offer to pay, understandably, since I was still interviewing for the position.

The job required that I move my family 2,000 miles across the United States. At the time, my daughter Maxine was 10 months old. I couldn't find a job here in Cleveland that was comparable to $90K in that specialized world of organizational development. OD is a niche and requires certain degrees, experience, and qualifications to do the work since, as I said, it is mostly a coaching training role; you are literally developing an organization's people and people leaders. I signed the offer letter and had a job description for Organizational Development Consultant, where I would be on the road traveling 25% of the time. I was perfectly fine with that because

I had always wanted to travel for work. My revised offer gave me $70,000. That was $20,000 less than the original promised amount of $90,000. ***First major ass red flag!***

It took me 90 days to get my act together, but we packed our bags and moved across the country so I could work this OD job. On my first day of work, they had another girl, around my age, with comparable experience doing the 4-hour facilitation job interview that I had to do three months prior. They also hired her on the spot. Later that day, on my first day of work, mind you, I was told I would no longer be doing the organizational development role but would rather be placed in the marketing department writing copy for marketing materials. Woah, wait just a minute. Firstly, that was not the job I was hired for OR HAD MOVED 2,000 MILES ACROSS COUNTRY FOR! Secondly, I had no marketing experience at the time, and I especially had no copywriting experience. I had never written a marketing copy before. Prior to this job, I taught college business courses full-time and am a doctoral-level researcher and writer, so yes, I was doing writing work, but it was doctoral-level research writing and not creative copywriting. I did not even possess a funny bone in my body at that time since I had the analytical brain of the PhD candidate.

I was in a state of shock. I am pretty sure I did rebut to some degree, but what could I do? I was a 28-year-old cisgender woman, and this CEO was my boss. He told me, and I quote verbatim, ***"I don't want you on the road traveling anymore since you have a 1-year-old daughter at home. You should stay home with her and work in this office."*** (Insert appalled face emoji!) I was stunned. Immobilized. No words even came out of my mouth. I ran to the bathroom and cried for 20 minutes, attempting to keep myself together and not make a scene in front of my new employer and colleagues.

Do you understand the weight and implications of his statement to me? Although I didn't realize it that day, looking back now with 20/20 vision, his statement was entirely sexist, derogatory, discriminatory, and predatory in nature. *He was literally discriminating against me for the following reasons:*

1. I was a woman (and a young woman under 30)
2. My baby was just 1 year old

I have worked and taught HR (Human Resources) since 2012, and you cannot discriminate against an employee based on age, gender, and parenthood, as in my case. I was discriminated against based on my age, my gender, and my status as a new mom. I was absolutely infuriated. I had just moved my family 2,000 miles across the country, leaving all family, friends, and my old college teaching job behind to work as an Organizational Development Consultant just for them to (on my first day of work) completely change my title and job description to Copywriter. They could have found A LOCAL COPYWRITER to work for HALF of what they were paying me. I was LIVID!

I got a PhD in Organizational Psychology just to become a Copywriter. What the actual f*ck? You do not need a college degree AT ALL to become a Copywriter. The OD role requires several years of experience, education, credentials, and qualifications. This was insane!

Couldn't they have at least had the common courtesy, decency, and respect (if they planned to change my title and job responsibilities) to call me before I moved 2,000 across the country and said, ***"Hey Alexandra- there have been some recent changes in our organization. We no longer need you as an OD Consultant, but we do need a Copywriter, and we wanted to offer it to you. Before you move 2,000 miles across the country and away from your family, friends, and job, would you like to consider this new offer or reject it and remain in Ohio?"*** Why wouldn't they have the common sense and respect to call and tell me about their change of plans? Instead of dropping the bomb on my first day of work when it was all too late. ***I would never treat someone like this! Ever! So disrespectful of them.***

It felt like I was sinking in quicksand. What on earth could I do? My hands were completely tied! I worked this bullshit copywriting job, but I sucked at it! Not on purpose, but because I was not a Copywriter! I had zero copywriting experience. I tried. I really did. I honestly put my best foot forward for this asshole employer, but I stunk at it. I was a doctoral-level writer. I was not used to writing at a 4th-grade level. There was nothing I could do other than give this company an honest chance. It was a conundrum.

After my first 30 days of employment, they let me go, saying it wasn't working out. Well, no shit Sherlock! They will get what's coming to them; karma is a bitch, after all. They gave me one month's pay as a severance, and we moved back home to Ohio breaking our rental lease. This entire experience was both catastrophic and traumatic for me. I was upset about this for months. I could have literally sued the shit out of them for both discrimination and a "bait and switch scam," but given my BIG HEART at the time, I decided not to. Yeah, that BIG HEART FOR BULLSHIT is long gone! *No more nice girl.*

I came back home to Ohio and, within months, founded Empower Human Potential LLC, which does exactly what they do: Organizational Development, professional coaching, and training. Today, seven years later, my organization is thriving and successful.

What is the moral of this story?

1. *Scams are EVERYWHERE!* Any business transaction of any kind has the potential to go south. Be very careful and always do your *due diligence.*
2. Always snag the job description and stick to it; employers use bait-and-switch tactics on employees all the time. Because the employer is paying you (and thus has all the power), they feel it is their right to use and abuse you, the employee. Look for red flags in jobs. *You are hiring them as much as they are hiring you.*

3. Karma will bite people in the ass who try scamming others. I am positive about this. What goes around comes around. You can't intentionally and unintentionally screw people over thinking you will get away with it. The **Law of Attraction** does not work like that.

4. This man clearly discriminated against me. I had the perfect legal case.

5. *When catastrophic events happen to you, such as 1) job loss, 2) break up or divorce, 3) death of a loved one, etc., just to name a few, usually that means you are leveling up and something bigger and greater is about to happen FOR YOU.*

6. I came home and founded my company in organizational development, which has brought me massive success, *making my first 6-figure sale two years ago.*

7. I would never have become an entrepreneur or started my own business if it wasn't for this idiot employer. Their buffoonery catapulted me into massive success and happiness. *I would have ended up employed by someone else for the rest of my life, incessantly making 5 times less than what I am worth!*

The most unfortunate events of your life are the most fortunate if you have the eyes to see them from that perspective. It is often when we drown that we learn how to swim.

The Biggest Fairytale Deception of All

My daughter goes to a private school, and although I love the school, they act like we do not work or have lives. They certainly do not consider single moms who do it alone with no help or support. Just this week, we have homework, two read-a-thons, three after-school events, spirit week, parent day, a whole school bookclub, 50 emails a day, and more paperwork. I felt like I was going insane keeping it all straight for her. Honestly, I threw my hands into the air. Not that I do not care about my daughter's academics, but 90% of what is thrown at me is bullshit, and it does not matter. I am not going to twist myself into a pretzel pretending to be supermom over here when I am running a full-time business. Jim Rohn says, ***"don't major in minor things."*** Something I previously did all the time. We do. We major in minor things. We focus on things that are not important. ***We focus on things that bring us misery and not joy. We focus so much on what we DON'T want and not on what we DO want.*** And then we wonder why we are sad, depressed, and disheartened.

The only things that matter are my business because that is my future and that supports us financially and my daughter's K-12 education because it will set her up for college. Spirit week doesn't matter, read-a-thons don't matter, the bake sale doesn't matter, parent day doesn't matter, the fall festival doesn't matter. It is just cluttering my already busy life. I must limit what after-school activities she does because I am the only chauffeur she has. I am not going to spend 80% of my time driving her around to this event or that event, this activity or that activity. I am not going to inundate my mind with clutter, bullshit, or things that stress me out, like spirit week and dressing her up like a damn clown every day. Our parents and grandparents were so hands-off when we were kids compared to what is expected of parents in today's world (2025).

They expect us to do backflips in the street naked for our children when, in our childhood, our parents kicked us out of the house to run around with the neighborhood kids for ten hours a day. Now, you can't let your kid out of sight for a second in today's world. But, have more kids, they say, so we can brainwash more people, create more mediocrity, less opportunity, more poverty, more Depression and despondency, and more people who spend their entire existence doing nothing but caring for others!

Caring for others is beyond noble, but it is not why you exist. You spend your life caring for your children, then your elderly parents and your spouse's parents, and you have no idea what it means to be a human being because your identity is so wrapped up in wiping everyone else's ass that you never realize your own ass needs wiping. The expectation of women in a caretaking role is sad beyond comprehension. Why? I know hundreds of women who have done nothing with their lives except care for others. I know what I am saying right now is offensive as hell and that caretaking is noble beyond comprehension, but give me a damn break; who made this shit up? Who deemed women universal caretakers while men can go f*ck off. Okay, sorry, I am on a tangent. Case in point.

You are not a universal caretaker; you are a human being. You were programmed to be a caretaker. You were programmed to be a baby breeding machine; you were programmed to be a self-sacrificing, noble beyond comprehension glutton for punishment. You are not sad and depressed. You were programmed to take so much on your plate that you have no other option but to be stressed out feeling anxious because so many people put so much pressure on your shoulders all the time.

Here is a deeper question.

Why does everything fall on the woman's shoulders? Has anyone ever asked this question?

If you want my opinion, it is ALL bullshittery.

As children, many of us dream of our adult life. No one pictures anything bad happening. It is all magical and imaginative as a child. You might have dreamed of your future family, future kids, future husband, future house, future career, white picket fence, family vacations, holidays, etc. ***You did not dream of the bullshit.*** You did not think about the hard work, the long days, the screaming kids, all the fights between you and your spouse, the endless laundry and dishes, the lack of help, the financial burdens, all the paperwork coming home from the school, all the grocery shopping, meal prep, and endless cooking. **You had no clue what emotional or narcissistic abuse is because fairytales strategically left out those plotlines.**

I cannot tell you how many women I know personally who are suffering through emotional/narcissistic abuse. It is so pervasive and still considered normal male behavior, which is strikingly shocking to me. None of this is normal. Treating your spouse like shit is not normal!

The biggest lie ever told to a woman is that she must submit to her husband. Nothing is a more compelling recipe for abuse and mistreatment. All people should be **self-governing,** making judicious decisions that give life and not take it away. All decisions either give or take life because all decisions yield positive or negative consequences.

Unlearn the bullshit and learn this instead – **you are powerful beyond comprehension.**

If you are offended, that is GOOD. **Have you ever analyzed and considered your social programming? Have you ever decided what is serving you and what isn't? Some of you were programmed straight into your abusive husband's home. Some of you have known nothing but a history of abuse and neglect, first in your home growing up and then in your marriage and relationships with men.**

If you are offended, that means that for the first time, you are seeing a clearer picture. You see these issues from a **different perspective**, which directly challenges earlier social programming.

Similarly, many of you were also conditioned to be poor and think like a poor person because concepts about money mindset are so messed up. You heard things like:

- ✓ Money doesn't grow on trees
- ✓ Look at how much I do for you
- ✓ The root of all evil is money
- ✓ Rich people are evil and bad
- ✓ Rich people don't go to heaven

This is how poor people think! Poor people consciously and subconsciously repel money based on their limiting beliefs about money. Money is just currency. There is a karmic flow to it; you must give to receive it keeping it in circulation. Maybe you saw parents waste money carelessly, or they had no money management skills. ***Money is abundant.*** There is so much to go around. You can reprogram your mind to think like a rich person, even if you are poor. ***Having money and making money is a mindset.*** You cannot fear money, and you should not be afraid to ask for it. Money makes people uncomfortable, which is why many people do not like sales; they have a hard time selling and asking for money. ***Decimate all negative and limiting beliefs about money; otherwise, money will never find its way to you.*** Open your hands up to receive money, wealth, prosperity, and abundance. Only you can determine what you are worth. Most people undervalue and undersell themselves for this reason; thus, they remain poor, and money remains an object for them.

Ask yourself: why do I think the way I think? Why do I believe in the things I believe in? Why do I value the things I value? Really dig deep peeling back the layers on the onion.

If you are hurting; if you are sad, depressed, anxious, deflated—***If you are powerless and disempowered, then check in on your social programming, early beliefs, and values.*** You can unlearn and relearn. You can be the ***black sheep*** of the family – you do not have to think like them or believe in what they believe in.

Sister –Stop chasing and start attracting.

Chapter 4 Takeaways

- ➢ Bad boys are very attractive, but they do not make good partners.
- ➢ Promise someone a fairytale, and you can influence them since most people's lives are boring. Remember, *everyone wants to feel.*
- ➢ Sometimes, *the only village you have is your own grit.*
- ➢ Motherhood is hard and a lot of work.
- ➢ Take notice of your *social programming.* Why do you believe what you believe? Think the thoughts you think? Value what you value?
- ➢ Scams and deceptiveness are all around you at every corner. Question and investigate everything. Even if your emotions get all worked up, do not fall for scams.
- ➢ *How does your childhood programming impact your adult life now?*

Share Your Story:

In the space provided, it is time to share your story. Think about the types of men and or personalities you are deeply attracted to. Are these people partners? Are they good for you? Are you attracted to toxic people or people who are good for your nervous system?

Chapter 5
Spiritual Awakenings

"Women have all the power at the beginning of a relationship, and men have all the power at the end of a relationship."

"Calmness is the cradle of power" – Josiah Gilbert Holland.

People either have a FIXED mindset or a GROWTH mindset. Those with a **Growth Mindset** are always ascending. Those with the **Fixed Mindset** are either descending or average at best. Anyone can tap into, cultivate, and manifest a **Growth Mindset.** It is available to all. ***Success and manifestation are incredibly easy; you just can't be lazy.*** Success and manifestation require **BIG ACTION.** That means you must get off your ass and stop making excuses. ***Once you begin, you will create momentum, which will turn into a snowball effect, and things will keep happening for you and won't stop.*** Many people do not even start, and that is their biggest downfall. Neville Goddard in *At Your Command* expresses manifestation this way, "Can man decree a thing and have it come to pass? Most definitely he can! Man has always decreed that which has appeared in his world and is today decreeing that which is appearing in his world and shall continue to do so if man is conscious of being man. Not one thing has ever appeared in man's world but what man decreed that it should."

Let me give you a practical example of manifestation in my own life. You can see how things naturally unfold and ***begin to snowball.*** Keep in mind, I started with NOTHNIG (which is a really GOOD thing).

4-12 years old – many dreams of flying ***(beginnings of ascension)***

2-12 years old – lots of time in reflection, exploration, imagination, wonder *(beginning of manifestation – visualization practices).*
11 years old – learned to read and loved it.
14-25 years old – turned my dreams of acting into reality. Worked on many plays, commercials, voiceovers, and indie films with A-list actors. Won several acting awards.
22 years old – graduated with my bachelor's degree.
24 years old – graduated with my master's degree.
25 years old – started teaching college.
26 years old – started my first business.
27 years old – did my first three-figure sale.
30 years old – graduated with my PhD.
30 years old – started my second business.
30 years old – did my first four-figure sale.
31 years old – did my first five-figure sale.
32 – years old – began writing the **GIRL GRIT** series.
33 years old – won my first business award. *Named Top International Empowerment Coach of the Year by IAOTP.*
34 years old – my first national keynote, earning a standing ovation.
30-34 years old – earned numerous certifications and published articles (over 50.)
34 years old – joined two book collaborations as a co-author, earning Bestseller status twice!
34 years old – made my first six-figure sale!
35 years old – **GIRL GRIT: SAVAGE NOT AVERAGE** was released internationally on November 8th, 2024, with Austin Macaulay Publishers.
35 years old – won 21 awards to date, 6 being literary awards for **GIRL GRIT: SAVAGE NOT AVERAGE.**

First seven-figure sale – TBD (insert excited emoji).

But... what if one of those suicide attempts had been successful?..........what if...

Let's assume I live to be of average old age, dying somewhere between 80-90 years old...that means I have approximately 50 more years to live! That is MORE TIME than what I have already lived! *If I achieved this much in 35 years, what will the next 50 years look like?*

Do the same thing I just did and complete a timeline of your life to date... you will notice all that you have achieved throughout the years, whether big or small, and how much more time you have.

Notice the pattern of ascension in my example, and the pattern of ascension in your timeline. THIS IS ASCENSION, SISTER! THIS IS WHAT ASCENSION LOOKS LIKE.

God/The Universe will strengthen you to do and manifest all these things that you really want to do. See how easy it is! *You just must do it.*

Laziness doesn't bless anyone. Get over your own bullshit and get on with it.

You have God's power to do all these things.

Birds are Messengers from God

I took a walk in the Metroparks on a normal day, got into my car afterwards, ready to head home with my car door still open on the driver's side. As I was fidgeting with my phone and GPS, out of nowhere, from precisely a 90-degree angle a bird shits exactly on my thigh with feces the size of a baseball splattered perfectly across my outer thigh.

I laughed and thought it was the most unexpected occurrence ever. *Hours later, I came to find out for the first time that being shit on by a bird is an omen of good luck and a sign from God that good things are coming your way. I immediately felt the presence of the Holy Spirit.*

This was a message from God telling me that I was about to embark on another Spiritual Awakening and that it was time to ascend higher.

Why People Blame God

People love to blame God. You have probably heard them do it a million times. You might have heard the following:

- *Why does God allow bad things to happen to good people?*
- *Why didn't God stop or prevent this or that?*
- *Why does God allow children and animals to suffer?*
- *There is no God, because if there were, he wouldn't have allowed this awful event to happen.*

Understand that God is NOT an ENTITY. Therefore, God does NOT ALLOW bad things to happen to good people, bad things just happen period! God is not human; God is a **CREATOR** with **POWER**. And that **CREATOR GOD**, who created you, bestowed upon you her **CREATOR POWER**, which means you have this **CREATOR POWER** too. Our lives are an amalgamation of high-highs and low-lows, which means that good and bad things will happen to you. **No one is causing good or bad things to occur; they are happening already as part of destiny. Furthermore, things only happen FOR YOU and not TO YOU, which means that even your traumas and tragedies happened FOR YOU.**

Let me give you a perfect example of this:

When I was raped, it was awful. Terrible. Traumatic. I am choosing to accept that it happened FOR ME and not TO ME. You might be thinking, how can rape be viewed in this more optimistic perspective? Well, I chose to bravely share my story in my first book, **GIRL GRIT: SAVAGE NOT AVERAGE,** because I realized rape happens a lot. It is something millions upon millions of women can relate to a greater or lesser degree, and those millions of women have probably remained silent about their rapes for a myriad of reasons possibly due to shame, protection of self and or violator, could have been a family member, too traumatic to discuss, or fear of discussion. I don't want these women feeling isolated or alone, as if it had only happened to them. *I encourage empathy and vulnerability with my readers because I believe my own healing will also benefit them.* Moreover, we need more education concerning the reality, frequency, and solutions for rape victims. I perceive all of this as a positive outcome. *I transcended my trauma into something educational and meaningful that would help others heal.*

Blame is also projection. People use God as a Scapegoat.

God's Power

Understand that because we humans live on this earth, we tend to think from a very earthly or what I call <u>surface-level understanding.</u> Things are not always as black and white as we'd like them to be. The universe is vast, and life continues beyond our earthly comprehension of earthly matters. *Our own pain and suffering, after all, is only caused by us and nothing else.* There are high-level spiritual realms beyond our human understanding and comprehension. *Most of us have not ascended past our own bullshit, which tends to bog us down in complete emotional suffocation day in and day out.* Ascended individuals think differently. They understand abstract concepts that an average person might struggle with simply because said average person chooses to retain a **Fixed Mindset** instead of cultivating a **Growth Mindset**. God does not have the mind that we humans have, so naturally, our worldview is rather limited and rudimentary.

Many spiritual individuals believe in our **Third Eye**, which is the Pineal Gland in our brain. This is also our subconscious mind. *Our Third Eye is all knowing and all powerful, but many of us have not tapped into its limitless powers; this is why many* *people choose suffering over ascension. They literally cannot see past the bullshit.* Don't worry, there is hope.

Humans are so powerful that it is frightening to consider. The reason you may believe that this is not true is because, for most of your life, those around you have been doubting, limiting, and disempowering you with lies and unproductive belief systems that have caused you more harm than good. For example, if you are suffering from Depression, you aren't really Depressed but rather **Disempowered.** Disempowerment makes you feel depressed, because disempowering someone is **LOWERING THEM,** while empowering someone is **HEIGHTENING THEM.** One reality makes something smaller; therefore, you feel small. The other reality makes something bigger; therefore, you feel big. *You have been lied to your whole life preventing ascension while supporting Depression, anxiety, negative feelings, worthlessness, and being "stuck" in relationships and professions.*

Because we are constructed by God/The Universe, she gave us her power, but most people do not believe this. They think God is higher than they, which is only partially true. Yes, God has a higher ranking because she came before you, but through integration and creation of your existence, *she filled you with her God powers. I will prove this now through scripture.* Let's look at some verses below. *PS – I am using she to reference God, but God is androgynous and should not have any female or male associations. I also use God and The Universe interchangeably as I am not supporting any one religion but rather pulling from various sources and beliefs defending my position.* It should be noted that this work is not a Christian nor a Buddhist work but is only using those texts as references.

1 John 4:4 "Greater is He that is in you, than he that is in the world" – *this verse suggests that God dwells deep within us, and if that is true, and there is integration with her embodiment, then naturally we possess her qualities.*

Mark 11:23 "Truly I tell you, if anyone says to this mountain, 'Go, throw yourself into the sea' and does not doubt in their heart but believes that what they say will happen, it will be done for them." – *This verse suggests we genuinely do possess God's power. If we believe, keyword believe, we can move mountains. Just touch things and they will turn gold. The difference lies in belief. Believing is also a Form of Divine power, because belief itself surpasses human comprehension, which is why many humans struggle with blind faith, believing without first seeing. You must believe before you can see. That is God's test to you.*

Matthew 7: 7 "Ask and it will be given to you; seek and you will find; knock and the door will be opened to you." – *The instructions here are evident. Ask, seek, and knock – that is all you must do. Do not overcomplicate a simple statement. Learn to ask. Ask for everything your heart desires. If you struggle with asking, I recommend you read the book, The Aladdin Factor by Jack Canfield. Most people struggle with asking, but asking and asking well is the secret to much success and happiness.*

2 Timothy 1:7- "For God has not given us a spirit of fear, but of power and of love and of a sound mind." – *This verse literally says God gives us power.*

Isaiah 40:29 – "He gives power to the faint, and to him who has no might He increases strength." – *Are you faint? Scripture says God gives you POWER. She gives you her God-like strength, which transcends human strength.*

Habakkuk 3:19 – "The Sovereign Lord is my strength! He makes me as surefooted as a deer, able to tread upon the heights." *This verse clearly expresses the power of ascension. God created you to ascend. She is encouraging you to ascend. You will "tread upon the heights."*

Acts 1:8 – "But you will receive power when the Holy Spirit has come upon you, and you will be my witnesses in Jerusalem and all Judea and Samaria, and to the end of the earth." – *this verse suggests that God gives us her holy power to affect change all over the world.*

Philippians 4:13 – "I can do all things through Christ who strengthens me." – **God gives us her power to do anything, literally.**

Luke 10:19 – "Behold, I have given you authority to tread on serpents and scorpions, and overall, the power of the enemy, and nothing shall hurt you." – **This verse says we are divinely protected because of our faith; we will have power over evil and the enemy. Death will not win, but Life will.**

1 Corinthians 6:14 – "And God raised the Lord and will also raise us up by His Power." – **This verse suggests that God is always raising us. We are continuously ascending.**

2 Corinthians 12:9 – "But He said to me, 'My grace is sufficient for you, for my power is made perfect in weakness.' Therefore, I will boast all the more gladly of my weaknesses, so that the power of Christ may rest upon me" – **this verse literally says, "the power of Christ may rest upon me." God's power is upon you.**

Colossians 1: 11 – "May you be strengthened with all power, according to His glorious might, for all endurance and patience with joy." – **We are strengthened with all power, but we must seize it.**

Luke 24:49 – "And behold, I am sending the promise of my Father upon you. But stay in the city until you are clothed with the power from on high." – **You are clothed with power.**

2 Peter 1:3 – "His divine power has granted to us all things that pertain to life and godliness, through the knowledge of Him who called us to His own glory and excellence." – **Her power has granted us all good things through glory and excellence.**

We are powerful. God has bestowed upon us her power. She has gifted us with power and has made us extremely powerful.

Chances are, you might not yet have activated or tapped into this power. It is very easy to do and requires only one simple thing: belief. <u>Believe you have this power. And so, it is.</u>

The Father of Lies

The reason you do not think you have any power is because of *the Father of Lies.*

John 8:44 says, "You belong to your father, the devil, and you want to carry out your father's desires. He was a murderer from the beginning, not holding to the truth, for there is no truth in him. When he lies, he speaks his native language, for he is a liar and the father of lies."

Many of us have been lied to for too much of our lives. We believed the Father of Lies, who cast fear, doubt, insecurity, disbelief, and negative feelings inside of us, disempowering and keeping us on ground level, descending into Hell with him.

We believed the following lies from the Father of Lies:

I am unlovable.
I am not good enough.
I am unworthy.
I am a failure.
I am an impostor.
I can't do anything right.
I am fat.
I am ugly.
I am stupid.

And so on.

These are **DISEMPOWERING BELIEF SYSTEMS.** They weaken you filling you with Depression and anxiety. These beliefs do not originate from God or the Universe. They come from the Father of Lies, who has been trying to destroy you since **he is a murderer.** For instance, many of you are in toxic relationships with narcissistic abusers. Narcissistic abusers do not possess the power of God; they possess the power of the devil, which is why many people consider them to be so evil. Narcissists are incessant and brilliant liars. They have you convinced that you are crazy, unlovable, ugly, worthless, useless, stupid, slutty, fat, unattractive, a failure and unworthy. **Yet, you stay with them because of fear.** Fear comes from the Father of Lies, and if you stay and do not leave, **YOU WILL CONTINUE DESCENDING.** STOP IT. ENOUGH IS ENOUGH. WE ARE DONE WITH THE BULLSHIT.

Matthew 20:16 – "So the last shall be first, and the first shall be last."

This verse suggests that the tables will always turn. It is another verse about power and ascension. Those less privileged, those with fewer opportunities and support, those with fewer resources will be first. **This is a Bible verse on motivation.** Those who start out in the world with less often become ridiculously successful compared to those who start out with more. When you start with everything, you feel no need to ascend, no need to improve, no need to break barriers, no need to overcome, and no need to work hard. Having a lot off the bat is very disempowering. **Those who struggle and suffer are extremely empowered.**

My Why

We all have a WHY. I want to share mine with you. As I have previously stated, I have spent most of my life with low self-esteem, lack of confidence, and unworthiness. I had my first thought of suicide at seven years old, along with seven failed suicide attempts in my teens. **I wanted to disappear.** The world would be better off without me. One night, I was Googling, yes, literally Googling **"painless ways to kill yourself."** And then suddenly, out of nowhere, a Bible verse popped up on the screen and said, **"For I know the plans I have for you, declares the Lord, plans to prosper you and not to harm you, plans to give you hope and a future."** Jeremiah 29:11.

*And I f*cking lost it.*

Plans? For me? Plans to prosper and not to harm? Plans to give me hope and a future? Me? **An unworthy human being?** The Father of Lies had me so convinced I was unworthy and that I was better off killing myself. He used others in my life to plant those awful seeds of unworthiness.

And just like that… I was healed… because words have so much power. At the time, I was just 16 years old. Today, writing these very words, I am 35 years old. 19 years later. **What if one of those suicide attempts had been successful? What if….**

We were not put on this earth to suffer; we were put on this earth to ASCEND.

If you do not suffer, you will not ascend. Do not be afraid of suffering. Suffering is not your enemy, but rather your friend.

When I was a little girl, I had incessant dreams of flying. I was always flying. **Flying is a symbol of ascension, a symbol of being close to God, of rising above your circumstances, and operating from a higher frequency and vibrational states, experiencing only positive emotions.** It is my dream, MY WHY, to someday travel the world internationally, speak, teach, coach, encourage, and build the **worthiness** and **self-esteem** in children, teens, and adults globally. This is MY WHY! **And it will happen someday soon; I am speaking it into existence now.** God will grant me **HER POWER** to make it so, because this is my purpose here on earth: **To tell every human being- you are loved, you are divine, <u>and you are worthy.</u>**

Sarah

My primary guardian angel is Sarah; she has been my guardian angel my whole life. She is an incredibly wise and powerful angel. An angel of strength and vigor, Sarah has a keen eye for danger, and she has protected me from terrible situations. Intuitive and all-knowing Sarah provides me with deep discernment and mastery in every area of my life. She is my guiding force of insight and protective energy.

An Introduction to 7 Known Archangels

You have both guardians and archangels guiding and protecting you every day. Learn who they are and the different types of support they offer you. Get into rapport with your guardians and archangels and watch how much they both guide and protect you on your spiritual journey.

Archangel Michael – Michael is the most powerful archangel. His armor is the Shield of Protection. He will keep you safe from all harm. He will keep you guarded, safe, and help support the healing and manifestation journey. Michael will keep you away from negative energy. Michael is very close to women who have experienced sexual violence and assault.

Archangel Rafael – Rafael is known for healing physical or psychological illnesses. He is the archangel of restoration and peace. He will keep you healthy and whole.

Archangel Gabriel – Gabriel is known for communication, often helping individuals gain clarity, discernment, meaning, and wisdom through writing and words.

Archangel Ariel – Ariel is the archangel of our environment, overseeing plants, animals, nature, and our ecosystem. Connecting with nature is a wonderful practice on a healing journey.

Archangel Jophiel – Jophiel is associated with beauty, creativity, and artistic expression. She will give you creative ideas and wisdom.

Archangel Azrael – Azrael is known as the archangel of death and the afterlife. He transports souls to the afterlife providing guidance and solace during the transition period. He also provides grief support when you lose a loved one.

Archangel Chamuel – Chamuel is associated with peace and courage. He is good to call on when struggling with anxiety and fogginess of mind.

The Magical Porta-Potty

These guardian angels and archangels are now your village. They will support you when your human friends and family are nowhere to be found. There are other ways you can call in help and support supernaturally. By connecting with the divine on a regular basis, you can manifest anything you want, literally. For example, I went to Washington, DC this past summer to visit my uncle. He showed me the different cities, including Alexandria, Arlington, Georgetown, DC, McLean, etc. We were driving down the streets of Georgetown in the pouring rain when suddenly I really had to go pee. There was no restroom in sight, only residential properties. I really couldn't wait; I was growing more and more uncomfortable by the second. I started to panic but instead called upon my guardian angels. Suddenly and randomly, about 300 feet ahead of us, a random porta-potty sat right in front of someone's house. As we pulled up to the porta-potty, the rain stopped. As I got out of the car, I ran to use the potty, then got back in the car. As soon as I got back in the car, it started downpouring again. *The heavens literally stopped the rain just so I could pee and stay dry for two minutes. **That is the definition of help.***

It is no surprise that we moms need lots and lots of help and support. Often, we don't get help, or we don't get enough of it. We can look for small ways to receive help from the divine and our spiritual guides. *Instead of panicking or going into a fight or flight, we can take a moment to pause, call on our guardian angel or archangel for guidance and support.*

Sister - You are a spiritual being. Open your palms to receive spiritual guidance and a spiritual awakening.

Chapter 5 Takeaways

> ➢ People have either a Fixed or a **Growth Mindset.** A Growth Mindset is necessary for ascension.
> ➢ You have always been ascending your entire life. As you keep growing and evolving, you will continue your ***ascension journey.***
> ➢ All your Limiting Beliefs come from the Father of Lies. You have been massively lied to.
> ➢ Birds are messengers from God.
> ➢ Annihilate disempowering beliefs embracing empowering beliefs.
> ➢ Life is held together at the cornerstone of the Power of Belief.
> ➢ God gives us her power, her **CREATOR POWER**. Scripture proves this time and again.
> ➢ Your guardians and archangels are here to lead, guide, and protect you always.

Share Your Story:

In the space provided, it is time to share your story: Identify your guardians and archangels. How have they guided, protected, and supported you on your journey so far?

Chapter 6
Believe in Miracles

*"The greatest miracle you will ever achieve is your own **self-healing journey.** The power we hold to transcend our pain is unheard of. By letting go of the past and the future, we soon realize that all the power we need to overcome anything exists inside of us right now at this very moment. **Your trauma is a gift, not a tragedy."***

"People are like stained-glass windows. They sparkle and shine when the sun is out, but when the darkness sets in, their true beauty is revealed only if there is a light from within." – Elisabeth Kubler-Ross

How to Easily Overcome Horrific Trauma

We've all been hurt. Not one person on the face of this earth has been without emotional pain of some kind. The dictionary definition of trauma is *psychological suffering and injury.* If you have ever experienced emotional and psychological pain, you have experienced trauma to a greater or lesser degree. *The intensity or impact of trauma can only be defined by the person experiencing the trauma.* One person's trauma is not more painful than another person's. For example, if person A's trauma comes from serving in the war and person B's trauma comes from childhood endangerment, you cannot argue which trauma is worse off, because the person experiencing the trauma or having the experience of trauma will judge and interpret that trauma at her or his own intensity level. Understand the different *Components of Trauma.*

Component 1 – THE ACT OR ACTIONS.

All trauma begins as an act or action that is committed against the person receiving the traumatic experience.

Example – rape. The act of rape is the physical act itself. It is the sexual violation of a person experiencing the trauma of rape.

Component 2 – The experience. The experience are the five senses "taking in" the experience of the rape. Rape is experienced through the five senses (vision, smell, touch, taste, and sound). *We experience everything in life through our five senses.*

Component 3 – The emotional response. The emotional response is the way we feel about what we experience through our five senses. The rape itself has triggered strong, intense, emotions within us. For example – during and after my own rape, I experienced feelings of *significant fear, anger, shock, and worthlessness.*

Component 4 – The consequence. The consequence is what happens after the traumatic event is experienced completely. For example – after my own rape, I experienced those intense emotions and thoughts of the different courses of action I could take. I chose to forgive and free my rapist writing about my experience in my first book, *GIRL GRIT: SAVAGE NOT AVERAGE.* Writing about my rape and educating women concerning the realities therein was the consequence (or series of events) that came out of my traumatic experience of being raped during a business dinner.

No human being is without emotional pain and trauma. *Being human by nature means the ability to experience suffering. Suffering is a universal human experience. Suffering is precisely what makes you human.*

When it comes to horrific trauma (such as rape or any other trauma, severity doesn't matter because severity of the trauma is subject to the traumatized person's own perceptions of reality) – *trauma can be OVERCOME.*

You then have only two options.

<u>**Option 1:**</u> Be overcome by trauma - never releasing those horrific memories and emotions, remaining captive of undesirable experiences.

<u>**Option 2:**</u> Letting go of traumatic experiences and transforming them into **personal power. You can take any situation and transform it into <u>something for good.</u> ANYTHING. You take it and transcend it into power.**

My rape made me a POWERFUL BADASS simply because I chose to allow it to do that for me. I transformed my pain into **potent purpose and power,** so that I could help women around the globe transform their pain, rape, incest and so on....

I am going to say this a million times until it sinks deeply into your subconscious mind... **YOU WERE NOT PUT ON THIS EARTH TO SUFFER; YOU WERE PUT ON THIS EARTH TO ASCEND.**

Pain will happen to you. You will experience trauma. No one is immune from these things; however, it is what **YOU CHOOSE TO DO WITH IT THAT COUNTS.** Let it go. Release it. Do not hang on to it.

Repeat after me...

I RELEASE MY TRAUMA

I RELEASE MY TRAUMA

I RELEASE MY TRAUMA

MY TRAUMA NO LONGER HAS A GRIP ON ME

I AM LOOSENING THE GRIPS; I AM LETTING GO

MY TRAUMA DOES NOT DEFINE ME

I DID NOT EARN MY TRAUMA

I AM NOT A BAD PERSON

I DID NOTHING WRONG

MY TRAUMA IS MAKING ME EXTREMELY POWERFUL

MY TRAUMA IS MAKING ME EXTREMELY POWERFUL

MY TRAUMA IS MAKING ME EXTREMELY POWERFUL

*MY TRAUMA IS MAKING ME EXTREMELY F*CKING POWERFUL*

Advice for Trauma Babies

A **Trauma Baby** is anyone who has experienced trauma before the age of 18. I want to reiterate that the only person responsible for your healing and emotional well-being is you, and NOT the people who hurt you. You must own your trauma as well as your ultimate healing journey. The **healing journey** can be long and sometimes last for many decades or a lifetime; therefore, it is essential that you consistently and regularly nurture and care for yourself. Here are some tips you can use ensuring you always get the love, care, and support you need long-term.

> - Always be gentle on yourself.
> - Prioritize yourself and your needs first.
> - Give lots of love, kindness, and compassion to yourself.
> - Practice self-care spending more time and energy on that.
> - Focus on your hobbies and interests pouring into those.
> - Listen to calming instrumental music often – this calms the nervous system.
> - Master the art of meditation for healing.
> - Take long walks in nature leveraging nature for healing and inspiration.
> - Use soft and dim lighting to ease your nervous system.
> - Always speak with a calm and centered voice.
> - Always give yourself whatever you need the moment you need it.

Why I don't Like Sin

I consider myself a Christian as someone who has lived by biblical principles to a greater or lesser degree most of my life. I extrapolate the teachings that bring value and make sense, and I release the teachings I find contradictory. *I do have a problem with sin.* As Christians, we are told that we are born sinners because of Adam and Eve and original sin. The day you are born, you are deemed a sinner because of original sin. You are born a sinner before you even commit any sins because of original sin. *Telling people that they are sinful or sinners suggests that they are bad. This idea of being bad or sinful is then imprinted on your subconscious mind and is part of your subconscious programming.* Telling someone they are bad or sinful *WILL ACTUALLY MAKE THEM SIN MORE.* Go figure. For me, the reverse is true. *We should be empowering people by telling them they are good, virtuous, generous, loving, kind, forgiving, and holy. This will make them do good.* Remember, the subconscious mind believes all suggestions AT FACE VALUE. If a person understands that she or he is a sinner, then she or he is likely to continue sinning because she/he is defined by the definition of sinner or bad person. *Conversely, if a person understands that she or he is good, noble, and virtuous, then naturally she/he is defined by those positive definitions and will continue to bring more goodness and virtue into the world.*

Bad exists in the world because we bring bad, whereas good also exists because we bring good. *WE EMBODY WHAT WE BELIEVE.* There is only one true sin in the world, and that is the sin of hurting someone else. Anytime you hurt someone else, you sin. That could be lying, cheating, stealing, false information, belittling, killing, raping, etc. *Anytime you hurt someone else, you sin. Hurting someone else only hurts you because it is a projection. You cannot hurt someone else unless ugliness exists inside of you.* If ugliness does not exist inside of you, then you will not hurt other people. It is that simple. *We cause our own problems and perpetuate our own suffering.*

Why People Commit Crimes – Where Evil Comes From

Have you ever asked yourself why your fellow humans commit ghastly crimes and where evil comes from? *There is no such thing as evil, but rather only traumatized individuals.* All behavior comes from a source. Such behaviors come from our emotions. That emotion is usually anger or sadness. The angrier a person is, the more traumatized that person also is. Crimes committed or one person hurting another is a release of those angry (feel bad) emotions, but they come at a high price. Children are the most vulnerable human beings, and because of society's great success at sweeping issues under the rug, most children grow up without a voice. *Instead of telling their story and sharing their hurt, they instead go and punish other people or essentially do to others what was originally done to them.*

I have carefully and thoughtfully delineated these specific childhood horrors in my second book, *GIRL GAME: BALLS OUT,* and I do not feel the necessity to repeat myself. However, in brief, it should be no surprise that a substantially disturbing number of children have been exposed both directly and indirectly to horrific and abominable acts at startling young ages. The younger the child is at the point of trauma, the more devastating the consequences. Childhood trauma comes in the following (common) forms, but I am sure this list is not exhaustive:

The most common, in my professional opinion, is *EMOTIONAL NEGLECT* (to a greater or lesser degree). I like to hope that parents do pay *emotional attention* to their children at least sometimes, but if this attention is not consistent as it should be, the effects are still emotionally neglectful, with some children experiencing extreme neglect and others minimal plus everything in between.

The second trauma is incest, which is far more common than what is accepted and believed in society. Some children are traumatized as infants and toddlers, let alone small children, older children, and adolescents.

Next comes verbal, sexual, emotional, and physical abuse of all kinds and conditions. The list is, unfortunately, endless.

It isn't always the parents who are the offenders, either. It can encompass other caregivers, siblings, cousins, extended family, neighbors, clergy, educators, and so on.

The point is, we are all capable of hurting other human beings **if we are unhealed.**

Most of the population walks around unhealed, which further perpetuates these unfortunate realities. I have spent years on the **healing journey** ensuring I have completely ascended above my pain and suffering.

Even in families where children thankfully did not experience abuse, emotional neglect could still very much be part of their reality teaching children to shut down their feelings. This explains why so many romantic relationships suffer.

Crime, evil, abuse, etc., are all a **purging of emotions.** That's it. Crime in this context, for clarification, specifically means (on hurting another human being) for instance rape, homicide, assault, battery, or **manipulation being the most common because it is the most subtle and harder to interpret/understand.**

I had a rather unusual thought when I was just three years old. I thought that if I were faced with a murderer, I could turn him around by changing his behavior by showing love and empathy. Now in my coaching practice, I turn around someone's despondent emotions within an hour. Using my tools and techniques, I know how to change thoughts, emotions, and behaviors in others, which today is what I do for a living.

Let's isolate the ideas of love and empathy. Murderers likely did not know love or empathy as children; quite the contrary. When love and empathy do not exist inside of you, because no one ever demonstrated those to you, you simply cannot give those positive feelings of love and empathy to others. It becomes impossible.

Our minds are incredibly ego-driven, where our brains attempt to protect us at all costs. By acting out ego-driven emotions, there is a sense of justice or release for our hurting inner child. This is why people hurt other people.

This is why war, homicide, rape, assault, and psychological deviance exist. No one is "crazy" for the sake of being crazy; *all insanity is born from insanity.* Remember that, prior to the past 25 years or so, people didn't openly accept or express emotions, so many were walking around like ticking time bombs with bottled-up emotions just waiting to erupt. This is why many fathers are yellers. Someone could spill a glass of milk on the floor, and these men will lose their shit. *Their level of anger never matches the crime.* What I mean is, spilling a glass of milk is insignificant because it can easily be cleaned up, no problem. When a man loses his mind over it, his anger is not justified because the crime (spilling the milk) was too minor in comparison. Because he has bottled up emotions, he is really releasing about 10 incidents in 1 sitting. These men and (oftentimes women too) learn to become reactionary. Why? *Because their fathers (and mothers) before them were also reactionary. All behavior is learned.*

When you are angry and reactionary, you are experiencing low vibrational energy. You will remain down and miserable until you learn to release all negative emotions, healing for good. *Healing is a process that does not typically happen overnight. It requires both energy and effort.*

If we can identify the root cause of the problem, we can effectively solve it. Many people live in a state of oblivion or complete unawareness of the larger and broader world. They are focused and fixated in their own bubbles. They bring about much suffering to their worlds both directly and indirectly. I know because I used to do this too. But understand, there is a larger world out there and much higher levels of thought, consciousness, and existence. We mostly just happen to live in a very worldly realm where we are accustomed to pain, suffering, and displeasure. This is why many people chase hedonistic and not eudaimonic happiness. Eudaimonic happiness is the answer to happiness. *Eudaimonic Happiness means meaning or a higher purpose; it is where we stop chasing after worldly existences and pleasures.* It is possible to live a happy, peaceful, *AND PROBLEM-FREE LIFE.*

I do! *I have officially divorced myself from all pain and suffering operating only from a place of complete worthiness and gratitude.*

To summarize, where does evil come from? *Evil comes from childhood because that is precisely where it is first learned and imprinted on the subconscious mind.*

Sister - You have the power to transcend trauma.

Chapter 6 Takeaways

> ➢ Life is happening FOR YOU and not TO YOU.
> ➢ You can transcend trauma through the **healing journey.**
> ➢ Healing comes when you are ready to let go of both past and future living entirely in the **present moment.**
> ➢ Awareness of pain and suffering is the first step in the healing journey.
> ➢ The only legitimate sin is the act of harming another person.
> ➢ **All crimes are rooted in childhood trauma.**

Share Your Story:

In the space provided, it is time to share your story: Have you ever been hurt by someone? Why do you think they hurt you? Have you ever hurt someone? Why did you hurt that person? Dig deeper and uncover the WHY in both scenarios.

Chapter 7
Are you Hiding Behind that Pretty Face

"An empowered, inspired, and confident woman will have all the guys chasing after her like she's the last woman on earth. But many of you walk around (head down), sad and insecure, incessantly seeking external validation. Let me introduce you to FIRE WOMAN. She's happy, she's empowered, she's fierce, she's free, and she lives inside of you and inside of me."

"Beware of what you set your heart upon... for it shall surely be yours" – Ralph Waldo Emerson

Are you Hiding Behind that Pretty Face?

He has the face of an angel. I have never met anyone like him before. Electric. Magnetic. **Dangerously good-looking.** Seductive. Charismatic. Mesmerizing. **Just looking at him made me want to cry.** After our unforgettable date, he got on his knees, grabbed both of my hands, looked me deep into the eyes, pulled me close, and said, ***"thank you, thank you, thank you, this was the best day of my life."*** He got up and opened the door and as he was leaving, I said, ***"absence makes the heart grow fonder,"*** as he turned around to look at me one more time he said, ***"yes, yes it does."*** <u>***After he left... I never saw him again.***</u>

I introduced **Electric Blue** in Chapter 15, *Wanted,* in my second book, **GIRL GAME: BALLS OUT.** The story of Electric Blue is a fascinating one and still undoubtedly the best day of my life – *a memory so fond I will remember it forever.* As you can imagine, I was devastated. Given his young age, I did not expect a relationship or a commitment out of him whatsoever, but I did hope to be friends, to build a lasting friendship that could draw us closer together. Afterall, it was his suggestion that we become **Affection Buddies. But friendship was out of the question.**

After our magical, awe-inspiring day together, I managed to reach out to him a handful of times over the course of 3-4 months, nothing serious, nothing insecure – I kept all correspondence "light and fluffy," meaning I kept my cool with him, not seeming desperate. I kept him at arm's length treating him like a friend, thinking I was playing it real cool. I didn't mention relationships, sex, or dates, nothing. I just sent him some funny memes and invited him to my birthday party in October and my Christmas party in December. I probably sent five text messages over five months, so probably about one reach out per month. **No response. Nothing. Completely ghosted. Discarded mercilessly.** At first, I thought something had happened to him, like something terrible. I couldn't imagine that he wouldn't reply at all or try to be friends with me because that was the relationship I tried establishing with him.

But he never replied at all. I was crushed. It took me months to get over him. I thought of him often, I pined over him routinely. That day with him was everything I ever wanted. *He made me feel alive. Wanted. Cherished. Loved. Valued. Seen. Heard. He made me f*cking feel. And then it was over with. No explanation, no communication, nothing, just blackness.*

I sincerely believed I would never hear from him again...

*That day was unforgettable, truly f*cking unforgettable.*

11 months after all that had happened, I woke up on a Wednesday morning with a text from him sent that night at 1 am, I was shocked. Baffled. I couldn't believe it.

His text read:

"Hey, I think of you a lot - I haven't been able to recreate our experience."

After I had been ruthlessly ghosted by him 11 months prior, I assumed that the experience we shared had only meant something to me because his silence had suggested it meant nothing to him. **But I was wrong.**

Let's analyze his text.

The first part of it is positive – "I think of you a lot." Cool. This suggests that I am on his mind, and he misses me. He has nostalgia and a soft spot for me.

The second part of it is negative – "I haven't been able to recreate our experience."

My question is – why would you try to recreate our experience with anyone other than me? Was I not good enough for you? Obviously not since you remorselessly ghosted me. You can never have the same experience twice, especially with another person. You cannot recreate an experience. **An experience is a magical moment in time. It is a gift from the universe.**

This statement still does not sit well with me.

My emotions got out of control. I became undone over reading this text. I cried those first two days simply trying to process my emotions.

I never thought I would hear from him again. My Electric Blue…

All my family and friends advised me to text him back right away, which is literally the worst advice in the world (sorry family and friends!) – they are not experts on Attachment Theory and human empowerment. They don't totally understand the dynamics and complexities of this situation.

Since Asher, aka Electric Blue, has an Avoidant Attachment Style, or at least displayed one with me, not giving them a taste of their own medicine is the WORST thing I could have done **because it would have automatically diminished my value in his eyes.**

Of course, I wanted to text him right away! It took every ounce of willpower and self-control I had in me not to do that. If you know anything about Avoidant Attachment Styles, Avoidants tend to play yo-yo with people's emotions. They get you, and because they got you, they discard you (once they get you, you become less valuable to them since they crave ONLY what they cannot have and do NOT appreciate what they do have) …. Once they get rid of you, they are elated…. for a while. A while can be days, weeks, months, or years, as that depends on the Avoidant and their unique intimacy needs. My Avoidant took 11 months. *THIS IS WHY NO CONTACT WORKS SO WELL ON PLAYING MEN – PLAYING MEN RESPOND TO NOTHING EXCEPT FOR BEING COMPLETELY IGNORED. YOU MUST BRUISE THEIR ARROGANT EGOS <u>WHEN THEY BEHAVE LIKE THIS.</u>*

In over 90% of cases, Avoidants almost always try to reengage, hence *The Cycle of Chaos.* I will not delve into *the Cycle of Chaos* at this time, as my second book, *GIRL GAME: BALLS OUT,* explores Attachment Theory in depth clarifying what the *Cycle of Chaos* is and how women become lured and trapped in it. The *Cycle of Chaos* goes something like this: *miss, idealize, devalue, discard, and repeat.* It is an incessant and ugly rinse and repeat reality where the Avoidant gets you magnetically attracted and attached to them using you like a plaything to be at their beck and call and *only on their terms* when they finally decide to miss you, and oh, they will miss you. This is where the saying "absence makes the heart grow fonder comes from." *Playing men grow cold and distant in your presence but miss and want you in your absence. It has to do with the Law of Scarcity.* People (especially playing men, more so) tend to only value, miss, desire, and want what they don't have *<u>because something rare is seen as higher value.</u> A woman who takes a man back when he comes back around is only devaluing herself and annihilating her value and self-worth <u>in his perspective.</u>*

Kelly from *GIRL GRIT: SAVAGE NOT AVERAGE* was advised to "take back her husband who returned home." She had a cow.

Never would she ever devalue herself like that by reducing her worth for someone too blind and stupid to see it in the first place.

Now, here is the conundrum. I am caught between a rock and a hard place.

What I want to do – text him back (emotional brain).

What I need to do – ignore the shit out of him (logical brain).

Every bone and muscle in my body wants to text him, but if I did, I would be lowering my value.

They say when Avoidants come back and you take them back, yes, there is a brief honeymoon period, BUT it is BRIEF. Significantly shorter than your first go-around with them.

This is the drug effect. **Avoidants are pleasure-seekers.** They are constantly chasing an **emotional high.** The chase is much more valuable to them than the catch. Avoidants cannot be caught. Let's use Heroin as an example. Heroin users are always "chasing the high," never fully getting the first high ever again. **This has the same effect in romance.** Sure, there may be a brief high, but it won't last at all. Once it's over, you are done and discarded once again, **and The Cycle of Chaos has spoken.**

You will be discarded again… harder and faster than the first time, and your value will be much lower in the Avoidant's mind.

Here is where things get even more interesting. There is a concept known as **the Laws of Power**, and you can leverage your **Dark Feminine Energy** becoming the unattainable, perfect woman he wants, but it requires **strategy.** Keen strategy. You must be slow, careful, and calculated. **Timing and patience are your greatest weapons in the battle of love.**

Put yourself into a position of power, because previously you gave your power away the first time, and that is why your Avoidant discarded you to begin with.

There can only be one person in power at a time, and it should ALWAYS BE YOU. You will not win by being in the opposite shoes.

Where does power come from?.... **Self-control and emotional grounding.**

What was the emotion I experienced when I first saw his text? **EUPHORIA.**

What did I do? I took a step back, no, sorry, I took five steps back.

I gave myself days to fully process all these crazy emotions his text message created. I did nothing except process my emotions. *I emotionally grounded myself.* His text message put me in a **HEAVEN STATE,** namely because he said and I quote, "Hey, I think of you a lot." To be on someone's mind a lot is telling. That means I am taking up headspace in his mind. He is obsessed or borderline obsessed (which is a good thing for attraction and desire). *To really hook and enchant a man, you need to get him to think about you 24/7.* How do you do that? *You f*ck him, not literally but mentally.* It's a complete and total mental f*cking because, guess what? *He did the exact same thing to hook you, right? Exactly.*

*Remember - <u>the best way to f*ck a man, is to NOT f*ck him (physically).</u>*

HEAVEN STATES never last long-term; they are usually very short-lived, which is why *emotional grounding* is non-negotiable.

I ruminated and ruminated. Truthfully and honestly, I didn't know what to do. I felt like I was in a damned if you do and damned if you don't scenario, but there was one thing I did know... I had the upper hand here. *I had all the power and control; I had Asher now at my mercy because I could either respond to him or not.*

At first, I thought of taking 3-4 days before I responded, but I realized the punishment did not fit the crime, after all, my prison sentence was 11 months. 3-4 days means he had one hell of an attorney. Then I considered a week – not painful enough. 2 weeks – maybe. 3 weeks, better still.

Listen to me closely – when it comes to ruthless, heartless, **playing men** who don't give a damn about you and your emotions, you must **DISH OUT TO THEM WHAT THEY DISH OUT TO YOU.** This is not a turn-the-other-cheek scenario. **You've got to stop being a nice girl, pushover, doormat, and glutton for punishment.** These **playing men** are flexing all their power and control over you. This suggests another vital Law of Power: **If you can make someone feel, you can make them do anything you wish.** These **playing men** have made you feel so strongly. They are able to control you and your emotions just like a puppet master would.

NOW YOU ARE THE PUPPET MASTER, SIS!

CAN YOU FEEL THE TABLES TURNING, BABY?

You must punish the man, you must. If you don't, he will never be enchanted, mesmerized, possessed, and transformed by you. **PEOPLE WANT WHAT THEY CANNOT HAVE – SO BECOME UNATTAINABLE, DAMNIT. YOUR WORTH IS NOT ON SALE AT A DISCOUNT PRICE!**

This man brought me to my knees, and still, I did not cave. **Why? Because I love and value myself more than I loved and valued him. I loved and valued him A LOT.** You have got to come first. **Your self-esteem has got to be more important than your emotions!**

This is why healing is a must. Once you heal, you will understand all of this.

Will I text him back? I think so. I am still in the waiting period as I write this. It has only been a week so far... not enough punishment, yet. I want to respond with something irresistibly witty and creative.

Deep. Enticing. Mysterious. Luring. Captivating. Punishing. And Reflective.

He will either respond to my text or he won't. If he responds, I will try and forge a genuine friendship (nothing more). If he doesn't respond, well, at least I knocked him off his pedestal and elevated my value in his eyes.

The most seductive thing is to friend-zone him because he will do everything in his power to get out of the friend zone.

Desire is all about creating pain. It is a push-pull strategy, **give some and remove some.** Your love, time, and attention SHOULD BE RARE. It should be earned and worked for; otherwise, they won't value you. **Playing men** don't realize what they have until it's gone – it's just a fact of life. I wish it were not this way, but it is.

This is not playing hard to get – this is playing hard to forget. Your value and worthiness must be so high that a man should be willing to climb mountains and swim oceans just to see you smile. Play their f*cking game. This is exactly what they do to you and why you find them so magnetically irresistible – it is simply human nature.

With that said. I may message him back, or I may not. I am still unsure. **The only thing I am sure of is that there will be punishment. He will get a taste of his own medicine.**

Women hold the keys to sex and men hold the keys to commitment. As the sex power position holder, never forget that... **the best way to f*ck a man... IS TO NOT F*CK HIM!**

It is the mental f*cking he wants and not the physical f*cking. He does not value the physical f*cking, but he does value the mental f*cking. **If you mentally f*ck him, which is what I am telling you to do, you will become a highly prized and valuable**

person to him. He will place you on a pedestal forever. He will NEVER fall out of love with or discard you. He will likely never even cheat on you (shocker!). You will become the perfect, divine, and holy superstar of a woman in his eyes. TOP-TIER WOMAN! FIRE WOMAN!

You are a FEMME FATALE – YOU ARE FIRE WOMAN - YOU ARE UNFORGETTABLE – AND YOU WILL FOREVER MAKE HIM WEAK FOR YOU…. FOREVER!

I have had men cry in front of me (in an emotional way) because I had my hooks so deep inside of them. I have had men roll out the red carpet for me and do backflips in the street naked. I have had men want to spend every waking second with me, because I treat them like this. I hate admitting this works, because it's borderline evil, honestly, *but no one ever got anywhere being a "nice girl" except for the psych hospital….*

You have got to own your power.

Do this… and you will never be discarded again.

There can only be one heartbreaker in a relationship; never let it be him.

Become the girl who is impossible to find. Become HER.

The Teacher

They say everything happens for a reason, and it really does. That is true. What I believe is this: *every person you meet is a teacher. They exist in your life to teach you something.* Even if they are only in your life for a short time, they will still reveal something to you about yourself that will help you grow. *Everyone you meet reflects you. They are staring back at you; you have both created and manifested them in your mind.*

For years, I was hiding behind my pretty face, not seen or heard. I spent the greater portion of my earlier life feeling invisible, after all, children should be seen, not heard, right? Or so we are told. *Asher made me feel seen in a way I had never been seen before, and that was through desire or <u>the feeling of being wanted</u>. Because I had been rejected in a myriad of ways in my life, I learned to reject myself. When I rejected myself, it was far easier for others to reject me, too. Meeting Asher awakened a spark in me.* He woke me up from a deep dream with clouds of unworthiness and confusion. *He taught me that if I didn't learn to love and value myself, no one else would or could love or value me either. He was simply a reflection of me.* He was only mirroring the beliefs (assumptions) I displayed toward myself. <u>*It wasn't Asher who abandoned me; it was I who abandoned myself. When I was a little girl, the seeds of unworthiness were first planted inside of me (by society), and since our subconscious mind takes everything at face value, I believed my entire life that I was unworthy of love. That unworthiness was made manifest.*</u>

But then, a miracle happened. For the first time in 33 years, on November 11th, 2023, at a motivational convention in a dark room filled with 10K+ other people, I accepted for the first time that I was a lovable *and worthy human being.* The speaker had challenged us to list at least 3 *Limiting Beliefs.* Since I am a Psychologist, I deemed that I didn't have any. I had already annihilated my *Limiting Beliefs.* The speaker encouraged us to open ourselves up and go deeper. I found one lonesome but potent *Limiting Belief* inside, and that was:

I AM UNLOVABLE.

Right then, and right there, he told us to annihilate our *Limiting Beliefs,* and so it was.

I came home a transformed woman – I annihilated my Limiting Belief that I was unlovable, and my entire world changed OVERNIGHT – LITERALLY. I received more love than I had ever received in my life. *Not only were all these men chasing me, dating me, spoiling me, but within a 2-month span, I had 6 ex-*

boyfriends / old flames return. One of them was my Asher, my Electric Blue, the man I thought I'd never hear from again.

If you are crying over a boy, it is likely you don't love yourself, or maybe you don't love yourself enough. *Bathe in an ocean of love and worthiness, completely surrendering all the old Limiting Beliefs of unworthiness.*

When you cultivate an *aura of worthiness* truly living and breathing it… I promise… you will never be discarded or rejected again.

<u>The only person who rejected you to begin with… was not them… it was you… they were just holding a mirror up to your face.</u>

<u>Asher was my mirror, and his ghosting me was saying, "Please stop rejecting yourself, you worthy human being."</u>

<u>And so, it was.</u>

BLOCKED

I honestly couldn't wrap my head around the emotions I was experiencing. The greatest emotion was shock. I was shocked that he had texted me. I was certain I'd never hear from him again. I waited two weeks to respond to this text. *For three reasons, 1) I wanted to increase my value; being friends with Desperate Debbie and Anxious Annie does not serve you. 2) I wanted to give him a taste of his own medicine for ignoring/ghosting me earlier on and 3) and this is the most important one, I wanted to master my self-control.* Just look around you and you will notice many people lack patience and self-control. Why is that? Even the fruits of the Spirit are love, joy, peace, kindness, generosity, faithfulness, gentleness, and self-control. In my opinion, *self-control* is the most difficult to master. We must control our thoughts and emotions. I did not want to be reactionary to the situation. *I gave myself time to reflect, meditate, and listen to guidance and direction while keeping myself emotionally regulated.*

Two weeks. I waited two weeks just to master my own self-control. After I had responded to his text two weeks later, I found out I was blocked. BLOCKED! Cut off. He's not on social media, so I had no way of ever contacting him again. I was devastated. As much as I coached myself to **not become attached to the outcome,** I was somehow very much attached to the outcome. He had given me a glimmer of hope to see him and reconnect again. I was just as shocked to find out I had been blocked; I was NOT expecting that AT ALL. He likely blocked me because he felt rejected by me since I waited to respond. His ego got bruised and he probably couldn't handle it. He figured the best way to forget I ever existed was to block me.

I lost control. I fell into a big black hole, the **Abyss of Misery.** I had done such a great job of emotionally and psychologically preparing myself to respond and anticipate his response. Once I knew I had been blocked unexpectedly, I gave way to fear, insecurity, abandonment, and devastation once again. I was devastated. I loved him so much. He and I both would have been far better off if he had never messaged me again. **I had already gotten over him the first time since he abandoned me, and now this reconnection attempt rekindled old feelings in me. I had to start the healing process all over again for the second time.**

Learning to Live

How could someone I saw only one time have such a profound impact on my life? **We only had one date together, but that one date was the best day of my entire life.** It was like a fairytale, a scene out of a movie. Something so rare and elusive. How? How could I love and desire someone so deeply who I had only been with for roughly 5-6 hours and then never saw again?

I knew the answer. *I needed to release him, heal, move on, and open myself up to receive my 10/10 person.* I didn't want to release him; I didn't want to move on. I was still hanging on tightly to him and those fond memories. We must let go. We must move forward. ***A train never goes backward; therefore, we must always be ready and willing to move forward. <u>Detachment is the most powerful weapon in your emotional arsenal.</u>*** In *The Seven Spiritual Laws of Success*, author Deepak Chopra says, "The Law of Detachment says that to acquire anything in the physical universe, you must relinquish your attachment to it. This doesn't mean you give up the intention to create your desire. You don't give up the intention, and you don't give up the desire. You give up your attachment to the result. This is a very powerful thing to do. The moment you relinquish your attachment to the result, combining one-pointed intention with detachment at the same time, you will have that which you desire. Anything you want can be acquired through detachment, because detachment is based on the unquestioning belief in the power of your true Self."

The One and Only Cause of Suffering / The Leading Cause of all Suffering

According to Buddhism and Buddhist theory, the number one or main cause of any type of suffering is ***attachment / longing / craving (the Second Noble Truth).*** Buddha developed something known as ***The Four Noble Truths,*** exemplifying that suffering exists in our world and it is simply a reality we must embrace.

The Four Noble Truths:

They are:

> **Truth 1** – Life is filled with suffering, and everyone suffers to a greater or lesser degree ***(suffering itself is inescapable).***

Truth 2 – The cause of suffering is clinging or craving (driven by the ignorance of reality) or hanging onto things that are *impermanent.* The stated cause of suffering is the desire for things to be different from how they are, which involves trying to change or control the outcome.

Truth 3 – One can let go of attachment and become free from suffering.

Truth 4 – The Eightfold Path is the path that leads to the end of suffering.

The Eightfold Path:

1. Correct View (understanding)
2. Correct Intention (avoid thoughts of attachment and other mental diseases)
3. Correct Speech (avoiding speech that is harmful to self and others)
4. Correct Action (do not hurt others physically, mentally, and spiritually)
5. Correct Livelihood (avoid harmful practices and behaviors)
6. Correct Effort (removing negative states of mind and embracing positive states)
7. Correct Mindfulness (*awareness* of body, feelings, and thoughts)
8. Correct Concentration (*focus* on things that matter and prosper)

Buddha was a great teacher who taught that we live in a world of impermanence or what I like to call <u>here today, gone tomorrow.</u> Most people do not like change, try to avoid it, and do not embrace it. **Change is constant and ever moving.** Things never stay the same for long. People often yearn for things to return to the way they were at the beginning, but that is simply impossible. In fact, it is impossible according to the laws of Buddhism. Things and people do change.

This experience with Asher taught me about life, attachment, and detachment. Meeting him and having that one date with him was one of the most exhilarating and profound <u>emotional experiences</u> of my life. I had to let him go. I had to heal. ***<u>He revealed to me what I was lacking within myself.</u>*** What I looked for in him was lacking in myself. He couldn't be the one to give it to me; I had to learn how to give it to myself. *That day with him was a gift from the universe.* A rare gift. A powerful gift. I wouldn't trade that experience for the world; it meant everything to me. But that is the thing about gifts; due to wear and tear, they slowly lose their value over time. Let's pretend I had 10 more dates with Asher, after each date, the value of the next date would lose some value little by little. *Since we only had this one date, it will never lose its value. Whenever I think of him, I will smile. I will have those positive, happy memories locked away in my snow globe.*

Today I choose gratitude. *I choose to be thankful for Asher. Although our time together was only a glimpse of heaven, the memory of it all was a profound moment in my life.* One moment of happiness is better than no happiness at all. *I have loved and have let him go, knowing he was part of my story but not part of my life.*

The Lesson

What could I possibly learn from this scenario? What good can come of it?

Gratitude – being thankful for what is/was and not what is/was expected. Do not be attached to the outcome. That day with him was a gift from God/the Universe. *It was just a taste or teaser of something <u>much more significant coming my way soon.</u>* It is as if God said, "If you enjoyed that experience, just wait for what else I have in store for you." *Be thankful for what was and what will come. See the bigger picture, knowing that your life is rich and filled with every blessing in the universe.* Our minds cannot conceive the grandeur of God and all she wishes to bless us with. ***Become <u>open for blessings,</u> open to receiving her abundance in her timing.*** Right now, open your hands moving them toward heaven. Release all past pain, hurt, and lovers. Open your hands receiving God's greater blessing in your life. Asher was only a taste of God's goodness, nothing more, nothing less. It is up to us **TO TRUST / HAVE FAITH** that we **DESERVE** all good things coming our way. If we have this belief, those good things will surely come. ***Wear your <u>Crown of Worthiness</u> every day. Many of you grew up wearing a crown of thorns of unworthiness, so you unfortunately attract people, situations, and things in your life that have made you feel unworthy questioning your worth.***

Remove the crown of thorns of unworthiness replacing it with your God-given ***Crown of Worthiness.*** You are beautiful and wonderfully made. God does not make mistakes. From here on out, if you still choose to wear your crown of thorns of unworthiness, you are insulting God/The Universe. It is a smack in the face to God's ***perfect manifestation,*** which is all that you are and all that you will be, and all that you are rightfully becoming.

I wore my crown of thorns of unworthiness most of my life. My head hung low, my spirit was despondent stung by rejection and oppression. I suffered and struggled so much, somehow surviving seven suicide attempts, with my first thought of suicide occurring at seven years old. Not being able to read until I was eleven years old…. ***But now every day I choose to be a WORTHY HUMAN BEING.*** It is a choice, and it is available to you, sweet sister. Make that choice and never look back. Holding onto fear, doubt, and insecurity is only crippling you. ***The reason you are in a miserable relationship is because of your own <u>perceived unworthiness.</u>*** Make that switch. Choose life, choose love, choose abundance, choose joy, choose peace, choose transformation, choose ascension, and choose worthiness. Choose you because you have been chosen by the Universe. What an honor it is!

Look at Psalms 46: 1-3 NIV– *"God is our refuge and strength, an ever-present help in trouble. Therefore, we will not fear, though the earth give way, and the mountains fall into the heart of the sea, though its waters roar and foam and the mountains quake with their surging."*

Just like the Hymn *It is Well with My Soul.*

Many things will not go your way. You will face endless battles, hardships, struggles, challenges, illnesses, heartbreak, disappointments, and horrible emotions. **It is called being human and living life.** Challenge and encourage yourself to say repeatedly:

IT IS WELL WITH MY SOUL – IT IS WELL WITH MY SOUL – IT IS WELL WITH MY SOUL.

Saying this means that you accept the circumstances for what they are, rather than what you wanted or expected them to be. You find joy and strength even in the most challenging and heartbreaking of situations.

Understand time the way God/The Universe sees it. My favorite description of time is found in Ecclesiastes Chapter 3.

Ecclesiastes 3 NIV

There is a time for everything,
and a season for every activity under the heavens:
a time to be born and a time to die,
a time to plant and a time to uproot,
a time to kill and a time to heal,
a time to tear down and a time to build,
a time to weep and a time to laugh,
a time to mourn and a time to dance,
a time to scatter stones and a time to gather them,
a time to embrace and a time to refrain from embracing,
a time to search and a time to give up,
a time to keep and a time to throw away,

a time to tear and a time to mend,
a time to be silent and a time to speak,
a time to love and a time to hate,
a time for war and a time for peace.

Ecclesiastes is my favorite book in the Bible because it teaches that life is vanity. ***All is passing away, and nothing is here to stay.*** In alignment with Buddhist teachings, it reminds us that ***nothing is permanent;*** all is continuously fading away. It articulates the prolific idea of ***impermanence*** and how we shouldn't hang on or attach ourselves to people or things. It reminds us that life is always moving and shifting, and if we are not willing to move and shift with it, we will accumulate troubles we don't want. ***The present moment is all we have. It is useless to dwell on the past as it has long since passed away.*** It is useless to live in the future because it hasn't happened yet. ***Nothing is guaranteed in life. You only have the present, so enjoy each moment for what it is and not what you wish it would be.***

How to Get Over a Beautiful Boy

If a man makes you weak, here is how you can get over him.

1. Let him the f*ck go. Seriously. Loosen the grips and let go.
2. Heal the parts of you that need healing – ***what exactly are you holding onto?***
3. Move on – there's always another dick out there.
4. ***Open your mind, heart, and arms up receiving the man who is perfect for you.***
5. ***Trust that your person is genuinely the best person for you and will not cause you harm.***
6. Embrace the theories and practices of Buddhism letting go of all earthly attachments and desires.

Sister – Detachment is your friend, not your enemy.

Chapter 7 Takeaways

> ➢ Men usually always return *(and completely on their terms).*
> ➢ Electric Blue was a representation of **impermanence** in my life, but he also served as a **blessing** and a **teacher.**
> ➢ All situations and circumstances are blessings because we can learn from everything we experience.
> ➢ Master self-control and the **Law of Detachment.**
> ➢ *All suffering is caused by an attachment of any kind.*
> ➢ It is possible to live a life **free from suffering** by mastering detachment and cultivating Buddhist teachings.
> ➢ *Impermanence is a fact of life.*
> ➢ It is possible to get over your attachments.

Share Your Story:

In the space provided, it is time to share your story. What are your attachments? What do you need to detach from?

Chapter 8
A Bite of The Poison Apple

"And he'll travel to the ends of the earth trying to find someone better than her, just to realize in the end that there was no one better."

"Everything you want is out there waiting for you to ask. Everything you want also wants you. But you have to take action to get it" – Jack Canfield

The Traveler

In my own experiences, it is not uncommon for me to find **Traveler Men.** These men are **classic chasers** or as I call **playing men**; they are incessantly chasing and never satisfied because the chase is far more exciting than the catch. **These Travelers are always on the move.** They don't stand still. They don't settle. Even Travelers WHO MARRY AND COMMIT still travel during their marriages; even though they are married and "settled down" legally on paper, they are still travelers, seeking and chasing other women. **Essentially, the heart of the Traveler is that they cannot be satisfied; <u>they are in a perpetual state of dissatisfaction.</u> Their sense of satisfaction is only satisfied through dissatisfaction and not satisfaction.** To a Traveler, there is no such thing as satisfaction, only dissatisfaction. Travelers are conditioned to chase and are conditioned to be unhappy. **Their happiness is unhappy, and their unhappiness is happy, hence all the chasing and traveling.**

Apathy – The Emotional Void

Electric Blue is a Traveler. He said in person to me that he experiences a lot of apathy. He mentioned that three times, which suggests that that (emotional state) of apathy is very apparent to him. Travelers feel a lot of apathy. **They are dopamine chasers, and those dopamine hits are extremely** *temporary, which is why they love you one moment and feel disgust for you the next moment once that high dies.* Apathy means coolness or lack of emotion and emotional excitement. It is like a void of emotions, which makes it very hard to connect emotionally with a Traveler. If you are not providing that *intense emotional high* that they are seeking, then they will tell you the spark died, and they will leave you. The question becomes, *how DO YOU BECOME THAT SPARK?*

FIRE WOMAN IS THE SPARK….

Electric Blue and I were two ships passing in the night; it was an experience I was meant to have. It was meant for me to experience and then write about in these books. I wrote a poem encapsulating this experience. It is called **Two Ships Passing in the Night:**

Two Ships Passing in the Night:

He lights her up; he makes her feel alive.
A showstopper he was with that electric smile and beautiful blue eyes.
Anytime she needs energy, she will call upon his spirit.
She doesn't believe in soulmates, but he was hers.
Like two ships passing in the night, a Smooth Operator,
He'll continue his traveler journey, always seeking to find her in other women.
Realizing only at the very end, he had her a long time ago.
Back in her day, she had bitten the poisonous apple,
And he was so delicious. Their feelings were the same,
But their experiences are so different.
Fade to Black.

A Universal Lack of Love

Many generations of people have systematically shut down their emotions. There is a great shutting down of emotions happening in our world, because some people view emotions as a bad thing. This is why men have been trained to suppress and repress their emotions, choosing to showcase only anger as an acceptable display of emotion. Therefore, there is a **Universal Lack of Love** which is equally experienced by both women and men. I have said in my writing many times that many children receive what I call ***obligatory or surface-level love*** from their parents and primary caregivers. ***Obligatory or surface-level love*** is ***not*** deep emotional love. When a child experiences this obligatory or surface-level love, it will feel like emotional neglect to the child, even though the parent thinks that she or he is not emotionally neglecting the child. It will be a feeling or reality the child experiences within themselves that is usually, to a greater or lesser degree, passed on to their own children decades later. ***The reason some parents love their children on a surface or obligatory level is because they are hurting so bad inside and have not healed their own trauma or childhood emotional abandonment issues. This prevents the parents from fully and completely loving their own children on a deeper level. The cycles of surface-level love are passed down generation to generation.*** This suggests that many people do not know how to properly love, and why, when the spark dies, so does the relationship. ***They are not truly loving, only experiencing egotistical emotions such as desire or longing, which is only created through*** <u>***scarcity, emotional unavailability, and abandonment.***</u>

Understand that rejection, heartbreak, and emotional abandonment are just parts of life. They are all low-vibe low-frequency energy. They are emotional forms of pain and suffering experienced in our physical realm of existence.

The Consequences of a Universal Lack of Love

The **Universal Lack of Love** causes serious consequences in our society. A few examples include, but are not limited to:

- School shootings
- Wars
- Abuse of all kinds

- Trauma
- Hate
- Division
- Crime
- Drug addiction
- Substance abuse
- Addiction of any kind
- Bullying
- Putting others down / Belittling
- Gossip
- Using people/manipulation
- Genocide

And so on.…

If we all loved better, we would all do better. It is that simple, honestly.

Sister – Love well, live well.

Chapter 8 Takeaways

- Be wary of **Traveler Men** and dopamine chasers.
- Parents of earlier generations remain emotionless and detached, causing suffering in children extending into adult life.
- Our world is comprised of a **Universal Lack of Love**, which explains crime and shitty human behavior.

Share Your Story:

In the space provided, it is time to share your story: Did you feel fully and completely loved as a child? Explain your story here.

Chapter 9
An Angel on the Beach: A Manifestation Story

"Everything that exists in reality today once began only in the imagination."

"What you think you become. What you feel you attract. What you imagine you create" – Buddha.

Pretending Comes First

Just like good things happen to those who wait, good things happen to those who manifest, those who create their own realities. I remember the day my entire life changed forever. I was 16 years old and had just had seven unsuccessful suicide attempts. I was hospitalized. I have shared this story in my second book, **GIRL GAME: BALLS OUT.**

You might remember my friend, the Faith Healer, the lady who transformed my life by speaking life into it. She only had good things to say, she only spoke life, and the miracle is… **I BELIEVED EVERYTHING SHE SAID, *and everything she said has come true.*** At the time, I was 16, I am now 35, she talked about me publishing books and being a famous author. At that time, I had no interest in writing or becoming an author at all, but she spoke it into existence and now I am an author, not because of her, but because of my own journey and what has led me here today. I have always believed in the divine powers of manifestation and have always been a manifester since I was probably just two years old. You might remember in Chapter 1 of my book **GIRL GRIT: SAVAGE NOT AVERAGE**, I shared the beautiful story about my celebrity crush. It seemed impossible that I would ever meet him someday.

I had a dream that I was at some sort of fan event and ran into him in the hallway, stopped him, and we chatted for a minute or two… that was the first time I met him, in my dreams. *The irony about dreams is that your subconscious mind has no disconnect between dreams and reality. What happens in your dreams is manifested in consciousness.* It must be so if you believe. I knew I had to meet him someday. I spent weeks Googling events to see if he'd be attending anything soon, but nothing. Nothing. He was attending no events now or in the near future. *That didn't stop me from manifesting a meeting with him someday.*

I spent hours visualizing it, praying, writing, everything you are supposed to do when manifesting. *The thing about manifestation is fourfold:*

In Manifestation

1. **YOU ARE A CREATOR** – you have this significant power, which over 90% of the population NEVER attempts to tap into. You literally create your own reality through your thoughts, feelings, and beliefs. Remember, your subconscious mind cannot take a joke, so whatever it dreams, it believes the reality of the desire has come to pass. Dreams and reality are one and the same thing, which is why people say, "my dream came true." *Dreams are a gateway to desire and manifestation.*

2. **YOU MUST ASK –** *Most people do not ask; therefore, they never receive.* Matthew 7: 7-11 says, "ask, and it will be given to you; seek, and you will find; knock, and it will be opened to you. For everyone who asks receives, and the one who seeks finds, and to the one who knocks it will be opened." This passage is extremely clear, ask and it will be given to you. *But most people do not ask… so most people do not manifest their desires.*

3. **YOU MUST BELIEVE** – the key to manifestation is not to worry about **the HOW.** If you worry about **the HOW, you**

simply have no faith. Manifestation requires complete and total **BLIND FAITH.** It is letting go of the control of HOW something will happen for you. **You must believe IT WILL HAPPEN FOR YOU.**

4. *BELIEF—I cannot stress this enough. Manifestation is a miracle but also an embodiment of your essence. If you feel drawn to a certain person (as I do my angel), that is because there is a connection there; my angel (this actor) reflects my essence to me. I am an ascended person. He is an ascended person. He mirrors my essence, and vice versa,* which is why I am magnetically drawn to him.

I let go. I relinquished control and I stopped searching for events, BUT I STILL BELIEVED I WOULD MEET HIM SOMEDAY.

I first discussed this story in Chapter 1 of my book, **GIRL GRIT: SAVAGE NOT AVERAGE.** The story appears at the end of Chapter 1, called **Pretending.** In manifestation, **the pretending part precedes the reality.** You cannot have a reality if you do not pretend it **already exists** first. **You must first believe that the thing you want has already been given to you, and you must be thankful for it. Pretending comes first.** I wrote about him in that book, I was already speaking things into existence because words, thoughts, and emotions have so much power. If you read that book, you might recall my pretend celebrity crush. Not to reiterate the entire story, but one of his Instagram Fan Accounts began messaging me while pretending to be him, and thus, we had a pretend relationship. If you read that chapter in the book, the rest of this will make more sense, as I would rather not retell the story again. I knew the impostor was not my actual celebrity crush, but I played along for the fun and for the manifestation. We remained close friends for over a year until I officially ended communication.

Last year, he messaged me (The Fan Account) still pretending to be the real celebrity **(I cannot bust him on his façade, it will ruin the magic),** so I played dumb. He told me he was going to this event in September and that I should come to it. I didn't believe him, so I just ignored the message. The next day, he sent me a flyer of the event and said that my celebrity crush would be attending for photos and autographs. *My jaw dropped to the floor.* I couldn't believe it, so I looked up this event online and sure enough, it was all legit.

Without hesitation, I bought my tickets, and three weeks later, I was on a plane to meet my celebrity crush, my angel. *Remember, I said you aren't supposed to worry about the HOW?* This is why people don't manifest. They get so wrapped up in the HOW, and all the HOW is doubt and fear. *If you have ANY doubts or ANY fears, then your dreams will never come true, because those doubts and fears are repelling and not attracting your desires.* You must have total faith; I cannot stress this enough. *You must annihilate all doubts and all fears.*

That Fan Account, that imposter pretending to be my celebrity crush, had served a significant purpose in my manifestation story. Because of him and our connection/messaging, I found out about this event. This event was NOT well-advertised at all. I saw it posted nowhere. None of his other fan accounts even posted it or advertised it. If it were not for the imposter sending me that flyer, I would have never found out about this event. Crazy. Crazy how God/The Universe can use an impostor to bring you to the real deal. How the fake brought me to the real. *How pretending brought me to reality.* The manifestation of meeting my celebrity crush face to face, in person.

The Letter

I wrote him a letter. It was heartfelt and succinct, and only three paragraphs. I started the letter by simply admiring his talent and on-screen brilliance, then I transitioned into briefly explaining how he has inspired me in a unique way. Those details I wish to leave out of this book because they are very close to my heart, but this actor has had a significant impact on my journey. I closed the letter with a call to action, putting the ball in his court, saying, "If you wish to write to me, I would love that." I added my phone number, email address, and business card.

I didn't know if he would accept my card and letter. I didn't know if he would even be allowed to. Sometimes these events have certain rules concerning what you can and cannot do. Regardless, I remained professional and respectful and didn't cross any boundaries. It was a 50/50 shot and a strategy. I could care less about this event; I was only there to meet him and hand-deliver this letter. ***I prayed he would accept the letter; I visualized him accepting it, and deep in my intuitive mind, I knew he would accept it.***

This event took place near the beach. I booked an oceanfront resort. This was the place where I was about to meet my angel in person. I had a connecting flight to my final destination, and when I got off the plane, for the first time ever, 1 out of 2 of my checked bags did not get off the plane with me. I was freaking out! ***That checked bag had the letter in it!***

I talked to associates at the airport to see where my bag was. It was on the next flight! She said that the plane would be landing in two hours and that my bag was on the plane. I had to sit there and wait for it. I was the only person on that flight who didn't get her bag. Everyone else got their bags and left. I had to wait for mine.

At this time, I was reading Neville Goddard's book, *At Your Command*. The book couldn't have been more perfect for this situation and manifestation. As I was sitting there and reading, waiting for my checked bag, I received an intuitive message. ***I was singled out.***

There would be 2,000 girls at this event who are head over heels for this guy. Those 2,000 girls represented all the people on the plane who got their checked bags and left. They met him, got their photos and autographs, they shared their stories and experiences on their social media, but they are not the ones. *I AM.*

At first, I was anxious and worried about not having my bag, but I quickly calmed down once I had the realization that everything happens for a reason and that this was a sign from the universe and a message I needed to hear. *I needed to be patient and wait.* The plane was an hour late; there was a Trump rally that same day in that same city, so the airport was all discombobulated as a result, which is why my bag never got off my flight. I had to wait three hours at the airport to meet this angel, but I feel like I would have waited a century just to meet him. The year was 2024, two months before Donald Trump won another Presidential Election. *What are the odds that a Trump rally would be happening on the day I landed in the same city? Another sign from the universe… synchronicity.*

When the 2nd plane landed, I got my bag, called the Uber, and headed to my Oceanfront resort. It was after 7 pm and I had to get up early, so I showered, ate a healthy salad, read a little, prayed, and went to bed early. The first 3-4 hours I couldn't sleep at all, I was tossing and turning. *My old familiar doubts and fears were settling in.* What if he doesn't take the letter? This is all so crazy! You are insane, this is all so impossible! *He's got millions of women who want him. What makes you think you are so special?* All my subconscious doubts and fears were reflected to me, and I couldn't sleep.

Eventually, I did fall asleep and had to wake up early to get ready. The next morning, my stomach was in knots. I was nervous but so excited. I coached myself through this whole experience. I said affirmations all morning while I was getting ready, mantras over and over and over. My main mantra was, *"I am a resilient and confident Queen." I wanted him to meet a Worthy Queen that day and not a scared, anxious little girl.* In Neville's book, he discussed the Grasshopper versus Giant concept. If you think of yourself as a little Grasshopper, then the Giants will seem big and scary. They will overpower you. If you see yourself as a Giant, then other people will also see you as a Giant. How you perceive yourself is how other people will perceive you, because they are only mirrors, reflecting to you what you already think of yourself. Instead of perceiving myself as a Giant, I perceived myself as a **Confident Goddess Queen** because I intuitively knew that my angel wanted to be with a **Confident Goddess Queen**. Many women do not walk around like **Confident Goddess Queens;** they walk around like scared, nervous, and unworthy little girls (Grasshopper mentality).

I felt inspired and empowered leaving my hotel that day and Ubering to the event. The event had only 2,000 people at a relatively small venue, much smaller than I assumed. Like I said, it was not well advertised, so the day went smoothly because it was a smaller, more intimate event. *I believed the day would go smoothly and perfectly, and so it did.*

My autograph was first, and the photo op was after. They segmented the auditorium and divided it into two sides: the far right and the far left. On one side, they did the autographs, and on the other side were the photo ops. *While I was standing in the autograph line, I saw him for the first time on the other side doing photo ops, and my heart sank; I was beside myself. THERE HE WAS!! (Insert crying emoji).* Then 20 minutes later, an Event Coordinator ushered him over to us for the autographs. I watched him walk over, getting closer and closer in proximity to me. *My heart was bursting out of my chest. None of this even seemed real. I had to be dreaming again. As he was walking, I literally saw an angel. A real angel.* It was him. It was really him. It was finally him, my angel.

Watching him sign autographs while standing in line was exhilarating. I couldn't believe it was him and that I was actually here right now in the moment. I looked around me at all the other girls, most of them under 40, a few crying, mostly everyone else looked scared (a nervous scared), no one looked happy, no one was smiling. I was surrounded by nervous Nellies. *There I was smiling, happy, laughing, jovial, soaking it all in.* I talked to the girl in front of me in line, and the girl behind me, and we formed a little group. They were both nervous and asked me questions, and so like I do, I started coaching them through the experience, telling them to breathe, be still and confident, be themselves, remain calm and diplomatic. Say what was on their hearts to say. They appreciated my *celebrity coaching.*

My heart was literally in my stomach. I was so nervous on the inside, naturally, but on the outside, I remained a resilient, Confident Queen continuing my affirmations in my head. What we believe in our minds is reflected to us in reality through *consciousness.* When it was my turn to meet him, he greeted me with a warm and gentle smile. As he was signing my photograph, I told him that he was a brilliant actor, and that he had inspired me on my journey. That I traveled all the way from Ohio to tell him this in person. He looked me in the eyes, and with the utmost sincerity, he said, *"Thank you, that means a lot." We locked our eyes for a whole moment in time, just like in my dream two years prior.* This was my *JUST F*CKING DO IT MOMENT,* thank you Ted (*GIRL GRIT* reference), I was scared and nervous inside, but I had to face my fears *head on* and *JUST F*CKING DO IT.* I told him I wrote him a letter expressing how he had inspired me. I asked him if he was allowed to accept it, *AND HE SAID YES AND HE DID! HE TOOK THE LETTER! HE TOOK THE LETTER. I AM SCREAMING, I AM CRYING, HE TOOK THE LETTER* (I had put the letter into a card)!

That was all that mattered was that he took that letter! It had my contact info inside (phone and email). *HE HAS MY PHONE NUMBER! I GAVE HIM MY PHONE NUMBER!* I traveled all that way to hand deliver that letter in person because there was NO OTHER WAY I could connect with him other than fate, other than a MIRACLE. I was flabbergasted… again. I couldn't believe it. ___The universe has an uncanny way of giving you exactly what you want, if you ask for it, and BELIEVE you will receive it.___

My heart was full. I had a two-hour wait before my photograph time, so I hung out and meditated on the experience I just had and how thankful I was that he took the letter. **The universe is working everything out for you.** ___All things happen in due course.___ Every wish and desire you have will come to fruition because you have the power to ask for it, claim it, and manifest it. Let's review my timeline so far.

1. I created an Instagram account to follow his fan pages.
2. I comment on his fan pages.
3. One of the fan accounts private messages me out of the blue, we start talking, and we become good friends, talking on and off for two years.
4. Almost two years after first speaking with the fan account, he sent me the flyer for this event. I bought my tickets.
5. My intuition opens the door telling me to write him that heartfelt letter.
6. I travel to the event and am singled out because my second checked bag never makes it—that was the first sign (of more to come).
7. *I met him in person, and he actually accepted the letter! That was nothing less than a miracle.*

I still cannot believe that he accepted the letter – what a miracle! He now has my phone number and email address. That's love, that is real love. I invested in this journey, traveled out of state, waited at the airport for three extra hours, lost sleep, waited in those long autograph and photograph lines just to hand deliver that letter to him: just to give him my phone number and email. That is what you call love, risk, and fearlessness. ___You have GOT to be so convinced that what you want more than anything already belongs to you, and you MUST___

He Remembered Me

When I got to the photograph line in the afternoon, it was moving much quicker, and they were swiftly photographing one fan after another. I continued my positive affirmations in my mind. *I remained centered, focused, disciplined, and worthy.* I am so deserving of having all that I want and then some. I remained calm and stable in my mind. *I did not allow my fears and emotions to overpower me; I simply dismantled them.* When it was my turn, I confidently marched up to him with the biggest, brightest smile, a confident and resilient Queen because that is the type of woman he wants. With a big bright smile, I said Hi and His Name. *He immediately lit up like a firework with his big, bright smile and said HI AGAIN in a warm and gentle manner; he distinctly remembered me from earlier at the autograph station.* We got our photo together, and he put his arm around the back of my waist and TOUCHED ME. After that snap, I left for the next person in line. My feelings were suddenly out of control. *HE REMEMBERED ME, HE REMEMBERED ME, HE REMEMBERED ME! Out of 2,000 girls, he distinctly remembered me. My heart was so full; a prayer had been answered, a wish fulfilled, and a dream come true. I was elated.*

How could it be so? How could I manifest one of the biggest and craziest dreams of my life? How could he accept that letter with warm and open arms? Sources told me he hadn't done an event like this in 6 YEARS! There was no formal way to meet him! Another source said that a year ago, he got asked to do an event and TURNED IT DOWN. Why had he said yes to this one? Only God knows the answer. This just means that nothing is impossible or out of reach. It is now in God's hands as to whether this celebrity contacts me, as I left the ball in his court, giving him the will and the chance to make a move. I am not impatient, and I am not sitting by the phone or computer waiting for the message. I BELIEVE he WILL message me. *I BELIEVE he already has, and I am GRATEFUL for it. I live only in the now, being thankful for each moment and every opportunity that comes my way.*

"Do not be anxious about anything, but in every situation, by prayer and petition, with thanksgiving, present your requests to God" from Philippians 4:6-7.

The only answer in the world is YES. No prayer can ever be answered with NO. Through the power of our thoughts, emotions, words, and actions, we will our desires toward either YES or NO, and according to our **FAITH,** it is done unto us.

"Then he touched their eyes and said, "according to your faith let it be done to you." From Matthew 9:29.

Do you know why people's dreams and desires DON'T come true? Because they are operating from a place of unworthiness (or worriedness or woundedness) and not WORTHINESS. They have little faith because we live in a society that has killed their dreams, so doubt and fear take over. **If you are consumed by doubts and fears, then your dreams will never come true.** You cannot operate like this anymore. It is robbing you of your magnificent personhood, and you are essentially MOCKING GOD! **You mock God when you hide your brilliance and creativity from the world.** She created you, and she wants to see those things become EXPRESSED, but you hide, and you suppress everything because you care more about what other people think of you instead of why you exist in the first place.

The only thing you even have is your own consciousness. Every person and situation in your life is a direct reflection of you, mirroring back to you **WHAT YOU ARE** and **WHAT YOU DO.** **Nothing really exists; it is only imagination in your mind.** You have created doubt and fear because doubt and fear DO NOT ACTUALLY EXIST. You made them up. You made them up, so they could sabotage you, because when you were a little girl, someone or something told you you were unworthy. You put on your crown of thorns of unworthiness every day, and it became another **self-fulfilling prophecy.** Do you have chills right now? And so, it is.

He replied, "You of little faith, why are you so afraid? Then he got up and rebuked the winds and the waves, and it was completely calm" from Matthew 8:26.

According to your faith, it is done unto you.

Think for a moment of all the winds and the waves you must rebuke in your life right now! In the name of **I AM,** together, let us rebuke these mighty winds and waves that cast doubt and fear clogging the **beautiful mind** God gave you. Say aloud now, I REBUKE IT, I REBUKE IT, I REBUKE IT. It is now gone, and it is no more.

Words carry so much power. You can literally talk yourself into any situation. For example, we had a community gathering, and one member was very afraid. She was afraid of getting sick; she was afraid of COVID-19. She thought that if she went to the event, she would catch COVID-19. No other member thought this, only her. The very next day, everyone was healthy, and she got COVID-19. **She literally spoke it into existence!** Remember, your subconscious mind cannot take a joke. **Everything you tell it; it must make it come true. I AM (your own consciousness) is everything.**

Isaiah 54:17 – "No weapon forged against you will prevail, and you will refute every tongue that accuses you. This is the heritage of the servants of the LORD, and this is their vindication from me."

The only weapon formed against you is you. You were created to have life and not darkness.

When I was a small child, I had only two types of dreams: nightmares and flying. One represented the past (nightmares), and one represented the future (flying). I am going to have enough audacity to say that most of us have experienced plenty of nightmares, especially as girls. Nightmares remain no mystery to women at all. For some of us, that is all we know. *You are meant to fly so high. Focus on flying. Focus on soaring. Focus on rising above all circumstances and all nightmares.* Paint these words on the canvas of your mind.

I KNOW is a statement of certainty. YOU MUST KNOW. YOU MUST KNOW. That all your wild, crazy, ridiculous, unbelievable, too good to be true, and out of this world dreams will come true.

When I was reading Joseph Murphy's book, *The Power of Your Subconscious Mind*, I was flying home from *Tony Robbins Unleash the Power Within, a live conference.* On the plane, sitting in first class, I was visualizing my angel. I was feeling all the good feelings and thinking all the good thoughts. After 30 minutes of visualization bliss, I looked over at the passenger sitting next to me and on his device, *I saw my angel!* He was watching a movie with him in it, and HE was on the screen the **VERY MOMENT I LOOKED OVER.** I was trippin'! I was beside myself. I burst into tears! The power of the mind is a mystical beast. Your mind does NOT know the difference between imagination and reality. Whatever you will, will come to pass. Do not WILL what you do NOT want. *Only WILL what you WANT, and IT MUST happen for you.* Cast out all doubt and fear. Doubt does not come from the divine; it comes from the enemy; *the enemy of the self.*

You can follow your dreams or follow the crowd—similarly, you can live your dreams or watch them die.

Both doubt and fear are CHOICES. Because you can CHOOSE not to doubt and not to be afraid. *I CHOOSE to have a beautiful life; I CHOOSE to be a success story.* Won't you choose together with me these things also for yourself? Once you begin receiving miracles, they will not stop. But if you give in to the winds and the waves, then winds and waves you shall receive.

Open the palm of your hands, surrender, and receive good things.

On August 14th, 2024 – a bird shit precisely right on my thigh inside of my car from a 90-degree angle. I laughed, not knowing what it meant, but knowing it meant something good. A day later, my aunt told me a bird shitting on you is a really good sign! It is a fortune of incredible luck because it is comparable to being struck by lightning. Even moreso, the bird pooped on me from a 90-degree angle since I was already sitting in the driver's seat of my car – even rarer! *After that experience, I felt the heavens opening to me.* It was time to ascend higher again. I experienced a *new spiritual awakening* because I was ascending into higher vibrational frequencies. My first book, **GIRL GRIT: SAVAGE NOT AVERAGE,** was being released (3 months later) to international markets, Walmart, Books-a-Million, Amazon, and Barnes and Noble. It all felt so surreal as if I had died and gone to heaven. Two weeks after the bird shit on me, my pretend celebrity crush from Instagram sent me the flyer to meet my real celebrity crush! It was through the **PRETEND (FAKE) CELEBRITY** that I met **THE REAL CELEBRITY. *It was my imagination that brought me directly to the realization. It was the PRETENDING that made the pretend a reality.*** Nothing is an accident. Nothing is a coincidence. Has it ever occurred to you that the worst, most traumatic circumstance of your entire life is precisely the power you needed to ascend? *Pain has transcendental powers. Your Goliath seems powerful, but it IS YOU who holds all the power and NOT your Goliath. Everything is reverse psychology.*

Matthew 20:16 says, "So the last will be first, and the first will be last. For many are called, but few are chosen."

What does this verse mean? This verse is about *reverse psychology,* and the tables always turn. It is also a verse about equality and leveling the playing field. "For many are called, **ALL OF US ARE CALLED. EVERY SINGLE HUMAN BEING IS CALLED.** But few are chosen." Only a small but very rare few of us are chosen. Why? Because only a few of us tap into this *personal power* we all have through *the power of our BELIEFS and according to our FAITH.* Men have always been FIRST for centuries, and women have been LAST. But now, the tables are turning. *WOMEN ARE NOW FIRST. Women – you who have put yourself LAST for everyone else, are NOW RAISING TO THE TOP and FIRST you shall be, for it is written in scripture and so it is.*

Miracles happen ONLY to those who BELIEVE in their POWER. According to the measure of your faith, it is measured back to you.

My First Miracle

I have shared my story a few times now. How I couldn't read until I was eleven years old, and how I was academically behind and placed into remedial classes in grade school. To a greater or lesser degree, I was told that I lacked (intelligence). I was consciously and subconsciously told I was dumb or that I was underperforming in relation to the other kids my age. *But the magical thing is, is that I did not BELIEVE those messages of academic unworthiness.* Something can only have power over you if you believe it has power over you.

As a small girl, my mind was always wandering into imaginary places. I visualized the most beautiful places I had ever seen. I saw fields of flowers in all different colors, sparkling streams of effervescent wonder, wild animals reveling in their freedoms, cities and towns so colorful and beautiful, strange and mystical places, rooms filled with books and knowledge, smiling faces and happy people, quiet, calm, and serene. *I flew everywhere.* I had a magical stick in every dream, and I couldn't fly without this stick. It was not a broomstick but a small branch from a tree. I would put the stick out in front of me as if it were a paddle board in the water with my arms straight in front of my chest. Within milliseconds, I'd be ascending into the limitless sky. ***<u>The stick in my dream is a representation of a FORWARD-MOVING DIRECTION.</u>***

Those with trauma tend to live in the past, constantly envisioning and re-imagining their traumatic experiences, so they remain and live with the trauma. ***All pain and all traumas must be let go of and transcended; once this happens, you will begin to fly. <u>Life is forward, onward, and upward always.</u>*** Life is constantly moving ahead and not backward; therefore, it is unproductive to live in the past torturing yourself with rewinds of old traumas.

Understand that ALL TRAUMA has a profound purpose in your life, no matter how god-awful it is. I was raped during a business dinner and within hours completely forgave and freed my rapist. It made me feel more powerful than I have ever felt before because only I had the power to forgive and free him and his transgressions against my personhood. May all women understand they are not alone. ***May all women fiercely and unapologetically share their stories with the world.*** May all women rise. May all women heal. May all women create. ***May all women ascend.***

That rape didn't happen TO ME. It happened FOR ME. IT IS TIME WE OPEN UP OUR MOUTHS AND SPEAK THE TRUTH INSTEAD OF BELIEVING A LIE.

STOP BELIEVING THE LIES OF UNWORTHINESS!

Everyone is a mirror in our lives, a reflection of us. He raped me because of my own unworthiness (still I did not deserve it), but my point stands. The truth is, he didn't rape me, only I had raped myself. ***When I forgave and freed him, I really forgave and freed myself for all those years BELIEVING I was an UNWORTHY and UNLOVABLE HUMAN BEING. All those years, I was laughing in God's face telling God subconsciously that she was a fool for creating me. It was blasphemous.***

It was because I couldn't read that I read.

That I earned a Bachelor's, Master's, and PhD, graduating at the top of my class with high academic honors, reading 4-5 books a month, founded two companies, authored this book series, won 21 awards (to date) and a million other blessings; *miracle after miracle.*

The FIRST shall be LAST and the LAST shall be FIRST.

You can be humbled and exalted at the same time, because all exaltation comes from humility, and they coexist in harmony. God herself has given HER POWER to you, for you are part of the master universe.

All pain has transformational power. I know you have trauma. I know you don't discuss many things that have happened to you. I know. BUT LET IT GO! Stop reliving the pain and suffering. Transcend! Ascend! FORGIVE YOURSELF. FORGIVE THEM. *FREE YOURSELF AND FREE THEM.*

There is NO SUCH THING AS BAD PEOPLE – only unwarranted and unhealed behavior.

We BEHAVE according to what LIVES inside of us.

For example:

If a good person who has good feelings and goodness in their heart loves and gives to others, that creates positive energy because good and love are being projected onto others. Good and love already exist inside of that person.

On the contrary, a person who has bad feelings and badness, hate, anger, grief, and unworthiness in their heart will create negative energy because that is being projected onto others. Badness and negativity exist inside of that person.

Anyone who criticizes, judges or gossips about other people has *low vibrational energy* in their hearts, and it is being projected out onto others. This will return criticism, judgment, and gossip back to the hater 10-fold via *The Law of*

Compensation / The Law of Karma. This is why you NEED NOT listen to those who criticize, judge, or gossip about you. *Trust me, they are judging themselves far more harshly because judgment is wedded deep in their souls.*

Let's understand the rapist and murderer for example. *Long before they raped and or hurt you, someone else raped and hurt them. They then raped and hurt themselves.* The idea of pain (hurt) got wedded deep into their soul and was then projected and manifested out onto you. This is why you must let go. **Why carry THEIR TRAUMA in YOUR SOUL?** Their trauma is not for you to carry. All trauma is passed on; thus, *trauma is cyclical. Trauma is nothing but programming of the mind, and as the mind can be programmed, it can also be de-programmed. The trauma can be deactivated. This is why trauma is a gift! It is a good thing! Just as all emotions are good and positive!*

*MY PAIN IS THE BEST F*CKING THING THAT HAS EVER HAPPENED TO ME. FOR WHO WOULD I BE, IF IT WERE NOT FOR MY PAIN, AND WHAT KIND OF POWER WOULD I HAVE?*

I want to see a world where women and men HEAL FOR GOOD.

For it is not pain that causes our suffering, but rather our EXPERIENCE of it. All experiences are profoundly positive and fruitful.

If there is anything I wish women had, it would be a pair of balls. Become more brave, fearless, bullshit-free, and powerful. But it will take balls! Have the nerve and the **AUDACITY** to challenge the status quo and say **ENOUGH IS ENOUGH!**

STAND UP AND TAKE CHARGE – BALLS OUT!

He and I

When I went to deliver the letter to him, it was only him and I in that gymnasium. Out of the 2,000 people there, no one was there. I had made them up in my mind. They were reflections of my own **subconscious programming** and my own **unworthiness,** telling me I wasn't good enough to have EXACTLY what I wanted. They were obstacles to actualizing my dreams and desires. Rhonda Byrne in *The Power* says, "As far as the law of attraction is concerned, there is only one person in the world – you! There is no other person, and nothing else, as far as the law of attraction is concerned. There is only you because the law of attraction responds to *your* feelings. It's only what *you* give that counts. And it's the same for every other person. And so, in truth, the law of attraction is the law of *you*. There is only you, and there is no other person. For the law of attraction, the other person is you, and that other person is you, and those other people are you, because whatever you feel about anyone else, you are bringing to *you*."

Sister – In due course alone, all your wishes, dreams, and desires will come true. Even the impossible ones.

Chapter 9 Takeaways

- Manifestation begins with **pretending. The pretend comes before the reality.**
- Your mind does not know the difference between pretend and reality.
- Visualizations are powerful.
- Believe that everything you want is making its way to you in perfect form.
- **You are a confident and resilient Queen.**

Share Your Story:

In the space provided, it is time to share your story. Tell a story about the time you manifested something you really wanted. What did you learn?

Chapter 10
Healthy Love

"There are four things no woman should ever put up with: assholery, bullshittery, buffoonery and douschebagery."

"What lies behind you and what lies in front of you, pales in comparison to what lies inside of you." – Ralph Waldo Emerson

Much of my writing has been comprised of what **unhealthy love** looks like, so in this chapter, we will be discussing what **healthy love** is and what it looks like.

Healthy Relationships

What are the qualities and characteristics of a **healthy life-giving relationship?** How can you identify patterns of behavior that will be good for you? **It is important to recognize and identify red flags as quickly as possible in a new relationship.** First, identify what you will and won't **tolerate.** Keep in mind that **what you tolerate, you will receive.** Make lists of your **green and red flags** watching closely for those behaviors. The best resource here is to rely on your **intuition.** Your **intuition** exists for a reason – TRUST IT!

<u>**Here are some relationship green flags:**</u>

- ➢ Regular and consistent communication
- ➢ No games (especially hot and cold)
- ➢ Reciprocity (give and take) – this one is HUGE!
- ➢ Listening well (active listening)
- ➢ Not interrupting the speaker
- ➢ Empathy
- ➢ Resiliency (no emotional reactivity)
- ➢ Asking thought-provoking questions
- ➢ Taking time to get to know someone

- ➢ Making efforts and initiatives – sharing thoughts and ideas
- ➢ Mutual planning
- ➢ Respect
- ➢ Honesty and openness
- ➢ Trust
- ➢ Boundaries
- ➢ Agreed upon expectations
- ➢ Discussing values, beliefs, behaviors, and ensuring there is alignment

Here are some relationship red flags:

- ➢ Love-Bombing
- ➢ Infrequent communication
- ➢ Sex pressure
- ➢ Shutting down
- ➢ Control
- ➢ Manipulation
- ➢ Taking (no reciprocity)
- ➢ Interrupting
- ➢ Only talking about oneself
- ➢ Not asking questions
- ➢ Not making efforts or initiatives
- ➢ Lying
- ➢ Cheating
- ➢ Façades
- ➢ Isolation
- ➢ Alcoholism
- ➢ Substance abuse
- ➢ Lack of respect
- ➢ Lack of boundaries
- ➢ Pressure of any kind

When it comes to dating, take the **hire slow and fire fast** mindset weeding out the bad eggs as quickly as possible.

ALL PEOPLE in your life will either......

*Support you or not
*Stand in your way or help pave your path
*Encourage or discourage you
*Give and take equally or just take without giving at all
*Be your champion or your enemy
*Motivate and inspire you or envy and sabotage you
*Promote love and well-being or drama
*Respect boundaries or manipulate you

Protect your energy, carefully selecting who is and isn't allowed in your life. It is perfectly acceptable and recommended to cut out people who do not serve a purpose toward life enhancement. Life is **The Law of Increase.** If they are **not increasing with you** and life is not mutually advancing with them, then it is time to re-evaluate. **We live in a society where being a glutton for punishment is no longer noble, necessary, or required.**

Relationship Alignment

It is known that people make decisions based on emotion and not logic. When we fall in love, we fall in love, and we base that decision of falling in love on emotion and not logic. **Falling in love is not logical.** Falling in love makes no sense at all, because it is a feeling and has nothing to do with **loving someone.** Loving someone is far different from being or feeling in love. Feeling in love is just a chemical reaction in your brain and nothing else, which is why it is easy to fall in love and easier to fall out of love. We get married because we have fallen in love. Men are more guilty of this than women because some women do marry for logic and choose well (even if not in love). Men, however, 9.9/10 times need to be in love or experience love for the woman in **feeling form.**

Most marriages end up in divorce because the couple is not **relationally aligned.** This means that likes attract like (The Law of Attraction). Many of our relationships do not align, and they end in divorce. All divorce, to a greater or lesser degree, has to do with relationship misalignment. **Partner up with someone where there is alignment.**

Alignment concerning:

- ✓ Religion
- ✓ Politics
- ✓ Lifestyle
- ✓ Raising kids
- ✓ Career goals
- ✓ Life goals
- ✓ Where you live
- ✓ How you relate
- ✓ How well you listen and communicate
- ✓ How you express emotions (or not express emotions)
- ✓ Entertainment
- ✓ Likes / Dislikes
- ✓ Preferences
- ✓ Tastes in movies, music, TV
- ✓ Sexual needs and preferences
- ✓ Household chores and domestic labor
- ✓ How you solve problems and make decisions

I could add probably 100 more items to this list, but the point is **RELATIONSHIP ALIGNMENT.** You will not be aligned 100% with this person because they are not a carbon copy of you. There must be enough **common ground** that it makes sense to even be together in the first place. When there is *relationship alignment,* you will know. Something will feel right, and if there is no alignment, it will feel off. **Trust that knowing. If a relationship is closely aligned, there will be minimal to no problems within that relationship at all.**

Spiritual and emotional alignment is vital when dealing with any type of relationship. Many of our relationships are **out of alignment.** When relationships are out of alignment, chaos, dysfunction, and disorder are sure to follow. *Let me ask you some questions to gain clarity.*

1. Do you come from a family of origin that did not appreciate or notice you? Did they fight incessantly? Was there always family drama and chaos? Was your original family dysfunctional in some capacity? Were you abused or mistreated?
   If you answered yes to any of these questions, your family of origin was not aligned, and to this day, they may still not be.

2. Have you had romantic partners you had nothing or little in common with? Have you had partners who were takers or abusers? Have you had partners who didn't support or uplift you? Have you had partners who caused trouble, chaos, or drama in your life?
   If you answered yes to any of these questions, your partnerships were not aligned.

3. Do you have friends who don't add value or meaning to your life? Do you have nothing in common with certain people? Are your values, beliefs, and lifestyles so dramatically different that you cannot see eye to eye on any subject? Do they have different hobbies and interests than you, and never acquiesce to doing something you'd like to do together?
   If you answered yes to any of these questions, your friendships are not aligned.

Alignment is defined by walking or moving in **THE SAME DIRECTION.** This does NOT MEAN that everyone must be EXACTLY like you. That is impossible. **However, oftentimes, we waste time with people and relationships who don't offer us much value.** I prefer friendships and relationships where we think alike, having similar interests and hobbies, and similar lifestyles. When this happens, it creates **alignment or congruency, building stronger bonds and stronger rapports.**

There are key people in my life right now who think nothing like me. We don't value the same things, and we don't hold the same beliefs (this is especially true for subjects like religion and politics), but can also hold true for life values, philosophies, beliefs, and ways of living or lifestyle habits. *I have respectfully distanced myself from these people because what they value and believe in contradicts my values and beliefs.*

For example, I highly value education almost to an extreme extent. Education is one of my top 3 values of all time. When I interact with people who don't value education or who are not educated, it is very HARD for me to relate to them and vice versa on any level or capacity.

The point being Alignment. The older I get, the more I realize how important this is. I don't come from money, privilege, or opportunity. I am an anomaly of the family. I no longer resonate with people without a **success and wealth-activated mindset.** I should continue aligning myself with successful and wealthy people since that is who I am and who I continue to become more and more every day.

There are four Levels of Love Interest, romantically speaking.

Four Levels of Love Interest

Attraction, desire, love, limerence, obsession, commitment, etc., are concepts of significant interest to me since I began my writing journey. It has been a few years now since I have found myself floating around in the dating pool, and from sheer observation alone, I concluded there are what I call **Four Levels of Interest or Four Levels of Interest in someone.** They are classified as **Level 1 (mild interest), Level 2 (moderate interest), Level 3 (intense interest / borderline obsession);** we can leverage a Level 4 and call **Level 4 appropriately (obsession with another person).** *Let me delineate these 4 levels for you.*

I have experienced all 4 levels concerning my interest in the opposite sex, and similarly, others have demonstrated these 4 levels of interest toward me also.

Level 1 – Mild Interest. This is the lowest level of romantic interest; therefore, it isn't very compelling. You are interested enough to talk to someone and possibly go on a date with them, but likely nothing further. Maybe there is something specific you like about this person that draws you in, but not enough to commit to seeing them often or developing a relationship. *You are unlikely to continue seeing a Level 1 interest person unless your interest in that person grows.*

Level 2 – Moderate Interest. In Level 2, there is more interest than Level 1 but less interest than Level 3. You probably wouldn't commit to someone in Level 2, but you might consider it if your interest grows over time. A Level 2 interest will probably take a few dates because you are interested in getting to know this person to see whether your interest or attraction in them increases. **You will put in more effort and prioritize this person over a Level 1 interest.**

Level 3 – Intense Interest. In Level 3, you are serious about this person. You think about them most of the day. You might not be obsessed with them, but it's close. You want to spend a lot of time with this person, and you certainly prioritize them over others. **They are your #1 choice/pick.** You put in extra effort attempting to see them at regular intervals.

Level 4 – Obsession with Another Person. You cannot get this person off your mind, no matter how hard you try. **They are all you can think about. <u>There are no others.</u>**

These **Four Levels** represent a **priority scale.** You will prioritize a Level 3 or 4 interest way more than a Level 1 and 2. Level 1 and 2 are usually placed in **backup categories** and are kept **as options,** although you would prioritize a Level 2 over a Level 1.

Love interests can both move up or down the scale at different times, depending on various factors.

Weaponized Incompetence

Women are notorious people pleasers, and this annoys me. Why? Why are women notorious people-pleasers, well, primarily because of our *feminine conditioning/social programming.* Remember in my first book **GIRL GRIT: SAVAGE NOT AVERAGE,** I dissertate that *women are taught to serve and men are taught to be served,* so in many, but not all cases, this creates a **physical handicap** in men, something called **weaponized incompetence,** whereby **men expect** services from women be it cooking, cleaning, caring for their children, washing their clothes, paying their bills, servicing them sexually etc. *This annoys me because it benefits men clearly and then punishes women, and the Bible has the audacity to say that men need helpmates. F*ck that, it is the women who need helpmates thank you. We are the ones doing EVERYTHING for EVERYONE.* Society annoys me because of social and gender-based conditioning. Yes, men can be people-pleasers, but usually, a man only becomes a people-pleaser if he must take care of his parents or younger siblings as a child, *but it is not quite as common as it is for women.*

Which brings me to my next point, **men do what they want to do, and women do what they don't want to do.** Think about that. What does it tell you? Women take care of everyone and manage everyone's lives, and men have **the freedom and opportunity** to chase other women and their dreams. **<u>This is why being a people-pleaser is not a noble quality.</u> The loss of yourself in service to others is not a virtuous way to live.** People pleasers are usually gluttons for punishment with low self-esteem. People pleasers have been conditioned to please people. *People-pleasing is not an inherent quality you were born with, and if it were, men would be people-pleasers too. But they aren't.*

Due to *gender social conditioning (and the glamorization of preferring male children over female children),* men assumed that they are the superior gender, and it spread like wildfire across the world, trickling down generation to generation and century to century. They gained an advantage by positioning themselves in roles of absolute authority while making women their helpers, or better said, servants. *A woman who lives her life in servitude is usually not a very happy woman, which could explain why Insomnia, Anxiety, and Depression are all more common in women compared to men.* Men have higher self-esteem overall because *they have strategically placed themselves in positions of advantage and authority.* Women accepted their places because they would have been burned or stoned if they didn't. They all became **conditioned to serve and please others. And people-pleasing was born.**

People pleasers are not respected people. You do not earn respect by people-pleasing; you earn respect by setting and commanding boundaries and sticking with them. That is what people respect. I am sick of seeing sad, helpless women with no self-esteem lacking a sense of authentic purpose. Here is my driving point – **NEVER GIVE TOO MUCH.** What does that mean?

Never give too much – love, sex, nurturing, service, money, or any other tangible or intangible substance. <u>You are a prized and rare commodity. Your love is rare. Your sex is rare. Your nurturing is rare. Your giving is rare. How can you ever receive if you overgive? You don't allow room for receiving when you give too much.</u> Robert Greene, in *The 48 Laws of Power,* discusses desire this way, "Desire often creates paradoxical effects: the more you want something, the more you chase after it, the more it eludes you. The more interest you show, the more you repel the object of your desire. This is because your interest is too strong – it makes people awkward, even fearful. Uncontrollable desire makes you seem weak, unworthy, and pathetic. You need to turn your back on what you want, show your contempt and disdain. This is the kind of powerful response that will drive your targets crazy. They will respond with a desire of their own, which is simply to influence you, perhaps to possess you, perhaps to hurt you. If they want to possess you, you have successfully completed the first step of seduction. If they want to hurt you, you have unsettled them and made them play by your rules."

Caring

We care too much about everything. **<u>You can only get hurt when you care.</u>** The secret to a massively happy and healed life is to **stop caring** (resilience). Literally, stop caring. ***Things are always happening FOR YOU; you do not need to maneuver any situations to get what you want; you are graciously and happily attracting all good things to you with <u>minimal effort.</u>***

Do not take anyone or anything seriously. Life is fluid and flowy; things are constantly in motion and always changing. Comparison is a thief of joy. Never compare yourself to anyone, when you do, you automatically self-sabotage. There is only one of you, and she is special, effervescent, and magnificent. ***Similarly, no one is better off than you. You were given all the resources to become massively joyful, fulfilled, and prosperous right now.*** In other words, look inside you. What gifts, talents, and skills do you possess that would be highly valued in the world bringing you ***exceptional fortune?***

Eggs in a Basket

Have options always and all the time. Never put all your eggs into one basket. Cast a wider net as I've said in **GIRL GAME: BALLS OUT**. You are an enigmatic **FIREWOMAN;** you do not need to be locked or tied down to any one man, especially BEFORE he has committed to you. Once he has committed and things are serious, then you can put your eggs in one basket, but before then, always keep your options open concerning love, career, opportunities, and friends. **<u>Never limit yourself and never feel limited by anyone or anything.</u>**

The Madonna and the Whore

Madonna and Whore Ideology is yet another way we cater to men and weaken ourselves as bold badass women. If you are unfamiliar with these terms, I will explain them to you. This theory *(Madonna versus Whore)* means that when a man meets a woman, he will *psychologically* place her into one of two distinct categories either the Madonna or the Whore. The Whore is a woman he will f*ck and leave, and the Madonna is the woman he will commit to and marry. **You must understand, this has nothing to do with you.** Meaning, there is nothing you are or aren't doing that is making him place you in either category. He does this *automatically* without much thought based on **HIS OWN PERCEPTION** of you and not your *actual value as a human being.*

The thing of it is, **he prefers the Whore over the Madonna**, but he would **never marry** the Whore, because in his mind, it would make him look bad in front of his friends and family. He wants to be **seen as a noble and virtuous** man with good taste. **He will only select the Madonna even though he is more attracted to the Whore.**

Let's break it down further, shall we? **What determines** a woman to be a Madonna or a Whore you ask? Mainly, **the difference between being a people-pleaser or servant** (The Madonna) or a **non-people-pleaser non-servant** (The Whore). This has nothing to do with sex, FYI. **Both women will have sex with him. It is just that the Whore has more self-esteem, and he psychologically knows that she is unavailable for manipulation and abuse. What good is she to him long-term? The Madonna can be categorized as a yes-woman or Trad Wife; she will both wipe and then kiss his ass when she is done wiping it.**

Please understand, this has nothing to do with your *actual value* as a woman and only to do with **how he perceives you.** For example, to Man A, you might be the Whore and to Man B you might be the Madonna. **It is all based on his perception and his** _**perception alone.**_ This is why it is important that a woman never becomes available to be caught. _**That she stands in her own divine worthiness every day wearing her Crown of Worthiness. Even if in a relationship or marriage, he should still never be able to catch you. Once you are caught, you will naturally be susceptible to manipulation and abuse, which is why many women are emotionally and physically abused by men. Comply or be punished.**_

On another note, the coming on of the sex. It is no stranger to us women how men can come onto sex so quickly and easily. Here is what I mean – you get on a dating app, and you match with a guy, and he immediately begins talking about sex and or sends you dick picks within the first day, first week or first month. _**Sex should not be brought up that fast; it is disrespectful.**_ He is either 1) testing you, so he can place you in the Madonna or Whore category or 2) he only wants sex treating every woman as a Whore and in that case, he would be called a _**F*ckBoi.**_

In summation, to playing men, we are either Madonnas or Whores _**but never full human beings,**_ which is why they don't regard us as such. _**Stop for just a moment and ruminate on who you could become if you surrendered love altogether.**_ I know you don't want to be alone, I don't either. _**But the fact that we need someone or need to find the one, or should get married, or this or that are just beliefs conditioned in us as children and teenagers.**_ We are all told, to a greater or lesser extent, that we need someone. No, we don't. _**What we need is a self. Self-esteem. An essential personhood.**_ You were put on this earth to do something grand, to make an impact, but some of you don't even recognize yourselves anymore.

Intimacy

What is intimacy? When I think of intimacy, I think of sex. _**Intimacy is the state of being intimate and intimate means close and affectionate with another person.**_ It is a deep understanding, appreciation, and softness for another person. *My own new definition of intimacy is seeing, hearing, listening to, and empathizing with another human being.* It is the essential and preeminent human connection. Moments can be intimate. You can experience intimacy with anyone, not just a romantic lover. You can experience intimacy with friends, loved ones, pets, nature, yourself, your art, etc. – it is seeing, hearing, listening to, and empathizing with another. *A close connection felt soul to soul.*

Sex

Sex is not about getting off. If getting off was the only goal, one could just masturbate making things simpler. ***Sex creates a need in us; the need to be seen on a deep spiritual and emotional level.*** Emotional neglect is very common in childhood, and we see this displayed in our adult lives. Emotions have only come to being in recent decades. What I mean is, back in your parents', grandparents' and great-grandparents' day, many people shut off or shut down their emotions. *Children were not allowed to express themselves emotionally. People were uncomfortable with emotions, and they became emotionally closed off, very stoic.*

With that said, many children grew up with suppressed emotions, and this is manifested in romantic relationships. *Anxious Pre-Occupied Attachment Style women get crippling anxiety over the men they love, and these men are Avoidant Attachment Style men with closed-off emotions.* The women are chasing the familiar; emotional unavailability they received in childhood. This is why they love and crave these Avoidant men. Similarly, the men run away from anxious women because *their anxiety and profound need for intimacy* are unfamiliar to the men. Men also experienced *emotional unavailability in childhood.*

These same men cannot resist avoidant women because the avoidant woman mirrors them. Not only is their commonality in avoidance behaviors, but the avoidant woman represents the man's avoidant mom and dad. He desires to win the love of the avoidant woman that he could never win from his avoidant parents as a child. ***This concurs with my idea of the Universal Lack of Love and the Universal Suppression of Human Emotions, which also explains our mental health epidemic.*** ***<u>If we were all loved better, we would all feel better.</u>***

That said, an avoidant woman will always be luckier in love than an anxious woman. An anxious woman has a **severe fear of abandonment** because she was (to a greater or lesser degree) **abandoned emotionally** in childhood. This creates a **self-fulfilling prophecy** in her life whereby all the avoidant men she loves **eventually leave and abandon her too. *If she doesn't love herself, how can anyone else love her?*** This is why it is essential to heal your insecurities and abandonment issues, or else the rest of your life will look like nothing but **heartbreak after heartbreak.**

Men and Breakups

In my life, I have been broken up with several times, and in all cases, it was because the guy **lost interest** or fell out of love with me. Whenever this happened, I would cry and move on with my life. Simple. ***<u>I didn't beg him to take me back ever.</u>*** I didn't act needy or desperate. I didn't act like a fool. I didn't stalk him. I just simply moved on with my life. I learned how to be rejected. Within the last year, I dated a man named Joe. Joe was a rather interesting case, and I will explain why. Joe and I had a total of six dates. I cut it off after six because I quickly saw his red flags, and I ran.

When I ended things with Joe, I ended them respectfully and diplomatically, being sensitive to his feelings. I sent a long message with my rationale giving him the opportunity to have a phone conversation to talk anything out, again, **out of respect for him.** Given it was only six dates, I didn't need to do this at all, but I didn't want to just ghost or cut him off. I have more decency than that.

As explanatory as my message was, Joe didn't seem to understand, so I further explained things to him in a polite and non-offensive manner. He did the worst thing he could have done. He attempted to CONVINCE me of why I should stay with him and not break things off. *Acting defensive, emotional, or desperate is the WORST THING a person can do in a rejection situation. He should have taken his dignity and walked away, but this man has no dignity, obviously.*

After another two weeks of convincing and incessant messaging, although I made my case crystal clear, I had to block Joe on text messaging and all social media platforms. He was not accepting the message that I was done seeing him. *He couldn't take no for an answer.* There was a brief period after blocking him (maybe two weeks) that I hadn't heard anything. When you are a dumpee in a relationship, the advice on the internet tells you to go no-contact, ideally for 30 days, but 90 is even better. Since Joe had no way to contact me, given that he was blocked, a few weeks later, he drove 90 minutes at night on my birthday delivering a bouquet of roses and a name-brand purse on my doorstep with a note that I discovered the next morning when I took my daughter to school.

Excuse me, sir, but you *cannot buy my love.* The note continued to kindly remind me what we "had" *(which in my opinion was nothing at all),* so I just ignored it. I will not be coerced or sold into being in a relationship with someone I do not want to be in a relationship with. I did not engage with Joe at all.

After not hearing back from me, Joe found me on Telegram and sent me a message, so I blocked him on Telegram. From there, he messaged my Facebook business accounts, so I blocked him on those. Since Joe had no way to contact me, he started creating fake Facebook, Instagram, and Snapchat accounts messaging me and further continued to harass me with loads upon loads of messages, which were not even coherent 80% of the time. The more I blocked Joe, the more fake accounts he created continuously engaging with me. ***This was total and complete harassment.***

I took the matter to the police, who didn't do anything except write a report and call him a few times telling him to "knock it off." The police were never able to get through to Joe, unfortunately. I did have a security system in my home, but it didn't have cameras, so I had to get emergency cameras installed in case Joe came to my property again. He also found a way to message a handful of my social media friends (all women) and harassed them. I found out because these social media friends of mine sent me screenshots of Joe.

Around this time, I received another gift in the mail from Joe. The gift was a photo album of all our pictures. The more I ignored Joe, the more he pestered me. ***His crime was incessant harassment after being told no repeatedly.*** After 3-4 weeks of this nonsense, Joe finally got the hint and gave up the ghost. ***He then returned two months later, asking for money on Cash App creating more fake social media profiles and phone numbers. Absolute insanity!***

I have a big problem with men in a relationship being portrayed as the ***hunters*** or ***pursuers*** of women. I absolutely detest the fact that it is ***socially permissible*** for men to hunt and or pursue me, but if I tried the same behavior, he would become turned off and run away. I have been told my entire life that women should never chase, hunt, or pursue men. ***<u>This reality makes me feel less than human!</u>*** Why are men allowed to pursue who they want, but I am not allowed to pursue who I want? It makes zero sense. ***<u>I have just as much will, drive, and sexual desire as any man does and in fact, I have more balls than most men combined (metaphorically speaking), so don't give me this bullshit about men are the hunters.</u>***

In the same vein, the other issue is men like Joe. *Joe represents a man who feels entitled to have any woman he so chooses.* He doesn't understand or accept the word no. He thinks that the more he pursues and chases me, the more likely I am to eventually acquiesce to his pursuit. He has probably been told his whole life that men are the hunters, chasers, and pursuers, so he cannot psychologically understand, appreciate, and accept rejection of any kind. It is a total and complete slap to his fragile ego. In fact, God himself probably told Joe I was his future wife. *Playing men thrive off this incessant chase.* The thrill of the chase, right? Once they capture you (if they do), it is game over for you; they have won, and then the fun and excitement are over, and they move on to their next conquest. *This is known as the Don Juan Complex.*

My best advice is to never acquiesce to the chase. Even when they "have" you, let them think they do, but always remain somewhat aloof and detached. This will psychologically keep them chasing you forever and in love forever. It is advantageous to be less in love with a man than he is in love with you. The one more in love always has less power than the one less in love. If you want all the power, then keep him chasing forever. Anytime I have fallen in love and acquiesced to the pursuit, it immediately ended, and the guy lost interest and broke up with me (Jordan from GIRL GAME: BALLS OUT).

Always focus on **YOUR VALUE** and always **KEEP YOUR VALUE HIGH**. It is easy for people to devalue you, which often happens unconsciously. Let me give you an example, if I may.

In my second book, **GIRL GAME: BALLS OUT**, I shared the story of my ex-boyfriend Jordan when discussing **Attachment Theory**. I was writing **GIRL GRIT: SAVAGE NOT AVERAGE** when I began dating Jordan. As an excited first-time author, I sent him a short one-paragraph excerpt from the book, and his *only comment and feedback* was that my writing was "cheesy." Cheesy! Cheesy means cheap and unconvincing. I remember being so highly offended by his remarks, but I dated him anyway. That comment (coming from a non-writer) devalued me. *Although offended, I proceeded with our relationship.*

GIRL GRIT: SAVAGE NOT AVERAGE won a 5-Star Book Award within its first three weeks of release, and *seven subsequent awards* within its first six months of release, so much for cheesy…

Never let a person devalue you, your personhood, or your work. What other people think of you is completely irrelevant and meaningless. The only thing that matters is what you think of yourself.

Foundational Relationships

Foundational Relationships are the closest relationships to us. Two prime examples include **Child + Parent** and **Partner + Partner** (romantic relationships). These are our closest relationships, **yet these are the relationships that usually cause us the most pain and suffering.** These are the relationships **that usually require the most boundaries.** Approach these relationships judiciously, diplomatically, and pragmatically. Prioritize yourself and your own needs first and foremost **(you cannot pour from an empty cup).**

Oftentimes, these relationships are toxic. You can work to make them better if they are workable, and all involved parties want the relationship to prosper. This would require **EMOTIONAL INTELLIGENCE** from all parties involved. **Without Emotional Intelligence, there is no prosperous relationship.** As advanced as our world is, to a greater or lesser degree, many people severely lack EQ. ***This is why so many relationships suck.*** For example, it is next to impossible to mend a relationship with your parents if they gaslight you denying that they hurt you in childhood. They refuse to understand things from your perspective, getting defensive and gaslight you if you mention any childhood trauma, abuse, or neglect caused by them. Same thing in a romantic relationship. If you call your partner out on hurting you (and they lack EQ and accountability skills), they will blame, gaslight, and deny you. This is the root cause of selfishness: ___the inability to understand another person's perspective.___

It is wise and practical to divorce yourself from such people. If that is not possible for whatever reason, establish strong, firm, and unyielding boundaries with them. **Pray for better and healthier relationships, and it will be given to you.**

Ask for anything you wish, if your heart is grateful, and your intentions pure, you WILL RECEIVE EXACTLY WHAT YOU ASK FOR.

WYD

WYD are my three least favorite letters when placed together. **Firstly, do not be a lazy ass.** You can type out, "What are you doing?" Secondly, WYD is **blatantly unattractive** and does not make me want to engage with or respond to you. Thirdly, **open your brain** and instead ask me a **THOUGHT-PROVOKING question** such as, "darling, what was your favorite part about today?" Or any other question that piques interest. Also, do not ask me how I slept or what I am wearing. I know you do not care about how I slept, and it makes you seem lazy again. **Open your brain and ask me a myriad of thought-provoking questions, so we can develop intimacy and an emotional bond.**

Medication

Medication is a band-aid. It helps you suffer just a little bit less by influencing the chemicals in your brain. **Taking medication, however, is not solving the root cause of your emotional problems.** Your emotional problems should be dealt with **HEAD ON. You are supposed to suffer?** Suffering is part of your human experience. On the same idea, you were not put on this earth to suffer, you were put on this earth to ascend. ___Before ascension can happen, the suffering comes first.___

Why We Cry

Crying is a release or purging of our *emotional world.* I call it an *emotional exorcism* as detailed in my 2ⁿᵈ book, ***GIRL GAME: BALL OUT.*** Crying is not a bad thing; it is extremely positive. ***Suffering is not a bad thing; it is extremely positive.*** Suffering means you are a real human being, congratulations! There is a secret I want you to understand: ***suffer strongly.*** Yes, ***suffer strongly.*** It is called ***productive suffering*** or ***meaningful/spiritual suffering.*** ***Suffering is the catalyst of ascension. It means you have the power to transcend your suffering.*** All suffering hurts. This type of suffering is no greater or less than that type. It all makes you feel like shit. It all makes you feel bad creating hell-state emotions. This is one primary reason why I don't believe in hell, because many of us are already experiencing hell on earth. ***Understand one thing, you created your own pain and suffering, which means you also have the power to uncreate it.*** To release it. To dismantle it. To destroy it once and for all.

How can you do this? Easy. ***We have the power to change our thoughts, emotions, and beliefs in a matter of SECONDS.*** Yes, seconds. It is through a process and practice called NLP, or ***Neuro-Linguistic Programming.*** I am not going to go into deep detail on NLP, but I will give you some basic information. ***Neuro-Linguistic Programming*** leverages the power of your five senses (touch, taste, smell, sound, and sight) taking information into your brain, which then creates your thoughts. Your thoughts create your emotions. And your thoughts and emotions create your beliefs. Your thoughts and emotions control your behavior, and so many of us feel powerless over our thoughts and emotions. However, NLP teaches us that the ball is in our court, and we have full and complete power and control over our thoughts and emotions influencing massive positive changes in our lives. In other words, it embodies an ***Internal Locus of Control*** (things we can change directly) versus an ***External Locus of Control*** (we feel like things happen to us without our direct control). It helps us change how we perceive the external world and our internal world. Just as a child, you were conditioned to believe this or that, feel this or that, or think this way or that. *You can choose to reprogram your thoughts, emotions, and beliefs to be productive and beneficial for you.*

For example, I only experience positive emotions 100% of the time. You might say, well, Dr. Elinsky, that is impossible! No, it's not because I do not allow the situations and circumstances surrounding me to influence how I am feeling internally. I do not allow my external world to impact or change my internal world. *I GET TO CHOOSE THE EXACT EMOTIONS I WANT TO FEEL MOMENT BY MOMENT AND HOUR BY HOUR.* Every day, I wake up and **DELIBERATELY CHOOSE** to only feel the **HIGHEST EMOTIONS,** which are *inspiration and empowerment*. I carry these emotions with me throughout my day, no matter what is happening around me, whether good or bad. I also CHOOSE to put on my invisible **Crown of Worthiness** every day so that I can attract more money, love, peace, prosperity, health, and achievement into my life. *It all keeps me focused and motivated to the maximum extent.* This is why I firmly believe that we create our own misery, and if you need to change something, then you have the power to change it.

For example,

If your relationship is hurting you – leave. *Let go of attachments; they are not serving you.*
If your job is taking a toll on you – get a new one.
If your friends always disappoint you – dump them and get new friends.

You don't have to remain stuck and miserable forever. You don't have to be a glutton for punishment. You can choose only positive thoughts and emotions, and you can change your beliefs too. *You don't have to believe everything you are told.* In fact, you should question EVERYTHING. Even the government, the news, authorities, science, and even religion. *All that matters is your own beliefs because it is your beliefs that create and cultivate your reality.*

Pain and suffering occur when you are out of rapport with your subconscious mind. When you are truly in rapport with your subconscious mind, you can command anything. Try it for yourself. If you are sick (and in alignment with your higher self), command the sickness away, believe it is already gone, and so it is. If you want a full night's sleep, simply tell your subconscious mind to get a full night's sleep. *It must listen to exactly what you command of it if you are in rapport with it and your higher self.* If you want to be massively rich and successful, the same thing. This will take work and action on your part with an *Internal Locus of Control*. That means you cannot watch Netflix every day and think that success and riches will organically come your way; no, you must get up and act.

For example, I want to be massively rich and successful, but not for egotistical reasons. I know that if I were to become massively rich and successful, I would use both my money and resources to do good in this world, being a force for good as I am already doing now. I will apply my money to creative projects that will help and inspire people to solve their own problems and live better, more abundant lives. My money and success would be used for the betterment of this world. I do *believe* this will happen for me because it is already happening now. Because you are reading my book, *I will give you a few of my top secrets or daily success habits.*

Daily Success Habits

Success Habit #1 – I bought a pack of GRE vocabulary cards on Amazon. Packs come in 500, 1000, or 1500 words. I study and learn 20 new vocabulary words per week sharpening my knowledge, expanding my vocabulary, growing my brain, and aiding me in becoming a more thoughtful writer and public speaker. This simple practice has had profound impacts in my life.

Success Habit #2 – I read 4-5 non-fiction books at a time consistently. I am incessantly learning. I read books written in the 1930s to the present day. ***Every author has something meaningful and insightful to say, and every author has dramatically improved my life to some degree.***

Success Habit #3 – I earn certification after certification. I take course after course. I earn an average of one certification per month.

Success Habit #4 – I do not watch the negative news. I do not care what is happening in the world. ***I focus on myself and my success so that I can bring positive change and transformation to the world, instead of watching mindless news so they can get more views perpetuating more fear in our minds.***

Success Habit #5 – I use social media only for business and not entertainment.

Success Habit #6 – I watch only 2 hours of TV per week for enjoyment and relaxation.

Success Habit #7 – I prioritize peace and mental health. I live a ***Zen Buddhist lifestyle*** where I am not running around 24/7 and busying myself unnecessarily. ***I spend significant time on grounding, meditation, praying, and reading every week.***

Success Habit #8 – I do lots of self-care, including regular massage, exercise, care of my body, hair, nails, dental, and bodily hygiene.

Success Habit #9 – ***I don't listen to other people or care what they think of me!!!*** They are only mirroring my own self-concept.

Success Habit #10 – I choose my friends and relationships carefully, spending time only with people who bring light into my life.

Success Habit #11 – I am careful who I take on as a client. I take only clients who are ready for transformation and willing to invest in a positive, abundant life for themselves. I do not take on complaining or whiny, ungrateful clients who drain my energy. These energy suckers give themselves away very quickly when you first talk to them. They are easy for me to identify and disengage with.

Success Habit #12 – I do not date men without *emotional intelligence* or who do not value personal growth and learning.

Success Habit #13 – Since I am a single mom with no help, I do not run myself ragged dragging my daughter to this activity or that activity. I am not a professional chauffeur, nor do I want to be. *I allow her to select 1 or 2 activities as that is my emotional capacity and limit.*

Success Habit #14 – I do not cook. I outsource my food. I do not participate in domestic activities that do not add value to my life. *Since cooking isn't making me money or building my dreams, I don't do it.*

Success Habit #15 – I am not reactionary. *I do not react to other people's bullshittery, buffoonery, unwarranted behavior, and hurtful actions, which are simply beneath me.*

I grew up with no self-esteem or self-worth. *It is now my hellbent vision and mission in life to travel all around the world, building self-esteem and worthiness in every human being.* I am not rich or massively successful right now, *but I am manifesting that.* The money will be used to accomplish these *life-giving goals* I have. *I am speaking it all into existence right now!* This is my intention, my purpose, my why, my magnum opus. I am sick and tired of seeing depressed, anxious, and low self-esteem people because it is all so unnecessary. None of us should live like that at all! You can be so much more. *You have so much power, together, let's tap into your limitless power and potential.*

If you have a want, wish, desire, or intention, do not worry about *HOW IT WILL HAPPEN.* How could it happen should NOT concern you. I am not worried about **HOW** I will become a billionaire. I just trust that it will happen someday soon, and it is only a matter of time right now and not will. I had to go through the god-awful, devastating, and horrific experiences I have been through to become the person I AM today. *I had to be dragged through hell. I had to be raped and abused and mistreated and bullied and rejected and abandoned. I had to have no self-esteem because how else would I be SO FERVENTLY DRIVEN to ensure that every human walking the face of this earth understands fully and completely without a shadow of a doubt that they are worthy, deserving, and lovable human beings? And THAT includes the homeless and incarcerated also. How?*

It wouldn't be possible. You won't know self-esteem unless you've known no self-esteem. You won't know worthiness unless you've known unworthiness. You won't know joy unless you've known Depression. You won't know peace unless you've known anxiety. You won't know love unless you've known rejection. You won't know abundance unless you've known scarcity. You won't know transformation unless you've known stagnation. You won't know heaven unless you've experienced hell. And you won't know EMPOWERMENT unless you've known DISEMPOWERMENT.

In **GIRL GRIT: SAVAGE NOT AVERAGE, Chapter 1 Starved for Love,** I shared my story of my celebrity crush. **Next weekend, I am GOING TO MEET HIM IN PERSON FOR THE FIRST TIME!** Your mind does not know the difference between imagination and reality. I dreamed that I would meet him in person, and now I am meeting him in person! Even I can't believe it. **BUT that is the power of manifestation! Not worrying about THE HOW.**

Don't worry about THE HOW. If you want something bad enough, set the intention and visualize it, know that it is already yours, and you will manifest it if you are in alignment and all internal blockages and limiting beliefs are removed.

The Universe / God opened the door to meet my celebrity crush. None of this was my doing – *it just happened FOR ME. Things are always happening for you. The good, the bad, and the ugly. Nothing is a coincidence. Nothing is without a divine purpose, even your trauma. You are supposed to suffer. The secret is learning how to suffer well by embracing and welcoming the suffering. Suffering is never permanent. Suffering is only an experience to be had and embraced.*

Sister - You deserve a healthy and life-giving relationship.

Chapter 10 Takeaways

> ➤ Learn relationship green flags.
> ➤ **Healthiest relationships are when both partners are moving in the same direction.**
> ➤ There are **four levels of romantic interest.** Level 1 of least interest to Level 4 of most intense interest/obsession.
> ➤ Playing men place women into **Madonna or Whore categories** – this has nothing to do with your **actual value,** but rather **their own perception of you**, which is flawed to begin with.
> ➤ **Emotional intimacy** is the cornerstone of a strong relationship foundation.
> ➤ **When a woman rejects a man, he should not try harder.**

Share Your Story:

In the space provided, it is time to share your story. What are the signs of healthy love? **Are you committed to healing so you can attract healthy love?**

Chapter 11
A Worthy Human Being

"A brave and resilient woman is a powerful woman. You were not born to hide; you were born to be seen, heard, listened to, wanted, and validated."

"He who has a why to live can bear almost any how" – Friedrich Nietzsche

The Power of Hathing

To **hath** or not to **hath,** *that is the question.*

Mark 4:25 KJV – "For he that **hath,** to him shall be given and he that **hath not,** from him shall be taken even that which he **hath.**"

Hath means to have. This Bible verse absolutely puzzled me for the longest time. In layman's terms, it means ***the rich shall become richer, and the poor shall become poorer***. I am sure you have heard that adage. From the external, this statement seems so unfair! How is it fair that the rich shall be given more and become richer, yet the poor, even what they have will be taken from them? It makes zero sense! Or does it?

I wrestled with the meaning of this verse for months until I was divinely inspired to write about it. This verse is **purely psychological,** and I challenge you to try **HATHING** for at least 30 days to see if it works for you. It surely works for me. ***Hathing*** is a psychological practice where you ***have in your imagination (hath)*** what you do not possess in reality (or 3D). For example, let's say I have $1,000 in my savings account, but I want to have **(hath)** $100,000 in my savings account. I will imagine **(psychologically hath)** the $100,000. ***Remember, that the imaginary or the pretending always precedes the reality.***

It is necessary that you hath every day. You can *hath* anything you want. There are no limits to *hathing*. I am now a professional *Hather* myself. I *hath* everything I want. When you *hath,* and you ***truly believe*** that you *hath* what you are *hathing* in your mind, to you it shall be given. You must believe (have faith), *hath* what you want to have. Start *hathing* now. *Hath* every day, all day. Never miss an opportunity to *hath*. *Hathing* ***will change your life. Hathing is a miracle.*** Wealth and abundance are mindsets. If you do not possess the mindset of wealth and abundance, then surely "from him shall be taken even that which he *hath*."

<u>You cannot have what you are not willing to hath.</u> The *hathing* comes before the having, always!

I challenge you to begin *hathing* now. Watch how your life magically transforms overnight. This is perhaps the most prominent theory in this book because "For he that *hath,* to him shall be given."

Playing Big Happy Family

Go on social media for five minutes, and you will note that every person on your timeline, to a greater or lesser degree, is playing what I call **Big Happy Family.** Most people like the idea of a **Big Happy Family** because it sounds and looks good. It is ideal. A pleasant thought. ***The reality is most of us do not come from Big Happy Families. Big Family Families are more of a façade than a reality because of the social masks we wear.***

To a greater or lesser extent, one can argue that many of us come from dysfunctional families. Dysfunction is defined in different ways and means different things to different people. What one family deems as normal and appropriate, another might call it dysfunctional, and vice versa. Normal and dysfunctional do not look the same to all of us. Every family creates its own normal and dysfunctional too. We can argue that every family is both normal and dysfunctional, depending on how you define normal and dysfunctional.

Everyone wears a mask. The type of persona they want perceived from the outside. *Many people are fake and phony, lacking authenticity, which is why lying and manipulation are so common.* Side Note: if I were you, I would learn about manipulation because it is so pervasive, and manipulators look for *easy targets.* When you arm yourself with knowledge about manipulation, it becomes virtually impossible to become manipulated again. Both women and men are manipulative, but it is more common for men to be manipulative toward women and for women to be duped because women are historically and transculturally conditioned to be *nice girls* (*Accommodation Queens*) who believe in so-called fairytales and *Big Happy Family*. Playing men use manipulation to get what they want because they operate from a place of *egotistical pleasures and gains* versus *wholeness and awareness. When emotions are involved and we are attached, we become susceptible to acts of manipulation.*

One of the reasons why women try so hard to save their marriages is because they want to keep up appearances continuing to play the game of *Big Happy Family*. If their marriage fails because of their husband's infidelity or other buffoonery, they tend to look inward and blame themselves. *Big Happy Family* is only a *perception* from outside of the family and not actually inside of it. Inside the family, there is a story that is much different, and happiness is (in many cases) not present at all due to addictions, alcoholism, abuse, antagonism, dissention, and the list goes on. Not only do we lie to society, but we also lie to ourselves, and worse yet, our whole lives become *one big fat giant lie*. Another term for this is *IMPRESSION MANAGEMENT.*

Impression Management means to directly and indirectly influence how other people perceive you as a person in your life. These so-called **Big Happy Families** are just *Impression Management* families. They will always have problems, but they don't want you to think they have problems because they hide their problems and sweep them under the rug.

For me, **I value honesty and authenticity,** and I hope my writing comes across to the reader as both honest and authentic. *I am a real human being, and I do not try to act like I am not.* I experience the same types of hurt and heartbreak that my readers do. I show my readers my humanity, so I share stories and examples from my own life, which I have done throughout this series. **What this world needs are for humans to become more human.** To embrace authenticity and not shy away from such realities. **Children grow up so hurt because it was more important to keep appearances than to be real expressing what bothered them.**

Develop an awareness of the broader world. There are many countries, cultures, religions, ways of life, and belief systems all over the world that differ from our own here in America. Our knowledge is so limited. Many people live in an enclosed bubble of limited knowledge and wisdom, which is why they continue perpetuating their own problems and thus cause misery.

Glamorizing and Idolizing Pregnancy

There are women who feel less than human if they cannot conceive a child, because as a society, we have placed such a ridiculous **idolization of pregnancy.** For example, as of late, I go to my Instagram feed and all I see is Gender Reveal after Gender Reveal reels. All the couples look like supermodels. The pregnant mom is always skinny and beautiful, and the father looks good too. They put on these celebrity-esque gender reveals that look like they cost a fortune. They lose their minds over the gender of the baby. People love to idealize and glamorize pregnancy and babies and then seem to lose the zest for it once the child begins to grow up and out of the baby phase. I have read in a book that there are some women who only love motherhood up until the child turns 2 years old and then lose interest or have another baby just to have another baby around. *In other words, the pregnancy and raising a baby (up to 2 years old) is significantly more valued and prioritized than the raising of the children themselves.*

This is just another idea perpetuating **Big Happy Family essentialism.** Women are adored for getting knocked up and popping out babies instead of bettering the larger world. I guess I cannot understand the big deal. Don't these pregnant women realize that they will end up doing the bulk of the childcare responsibilities with or without the baby's dad's help and support? Sure, being pregnant is fun. Sure, having a baby is fun, but when it comes time to raising that child my goodness it's exhausting, thankless, unappreciated, time-consuming, and sometimes just a damn headache.

Pregnancy becomes hedonistic in nature. It's so exciting, but that excitement is only temporary, and then reality kicks in sooner or later. Yes, some fathers are involved, and they do help, but I would be remiss if I didn't note how many do not pull their fair share, and the women do it all alone. Somehow, it becomes almost exclusively a woman's responsibility. *Find something other than a baby to give birth to.*

The Great Suppression

As a **Social Justice Warrior** using the gift of my **intuition,** I often see patterns of human behavior that exist in our world. Through **recognition** and **social awareness**, we can identify these **problematic patterns** beginning to resolve the issues. You have heard of The Great Depression, which began in 1929, but you haven't heard of **THE GREAT SUPPRESSION**, which is my term. *The Great Suppression is the systemic removal or mitigation of our essence or essential personhood.* What this means is that society collectively does a fine job of encouraging us to **suppress instead of express** ourselves. *The ones who*

We have all been taught that it is **wrong to brag**. Bragging is the **enthusiastic expression** or sharing of our accomplishments and greatness, which is positioned in a negative perspective in society. Most people curtail their achievements and accomplishments because they don't want to be categorized as boastful. Perception is the way you view something. **What if we changed the narrative? What if we encouraged people to brag? I don't know about you, but I love to celebrate, encourage, support, and champion other people.** It is just who I am. If I see you post an accomplishment on social media, I will comment on and praise you for it, lifting your energetic vibrations. When I post accomplishments on social media, I may get anywhere from 5-70 likes depending on the accomplishment, but if I post anything about being a mother or post photos of my kid, I will get 100+ likes like clockwork. Why is this? **<u>Because women are praised more for being mothers than they are for achieving anything else outside of motherhood. People are afraid of what women might become.</u>**

<u>How are we supposed to become successful if we are programmed to believe that no one really wants to see us win?</u>

This is why women hate on each other. Women antagonize other women and hate seeing them win, because women are told they are not allowed to excel and achieve. If they do, not too big, you shouldn't outshine anyone especially your kids or man.

<u>We learn as women that we don't really matter at all, and that we just exist to wipe everyone's ass expect for our own.</u>

The Great Elevation

This is called The Great Suppression, because we are taught to hide our brilliance from the world. When we hide our brilliance from the world, we laugh in God's face. You are basically calling your maker a fool because you don't believe that her creation, which is YOU, is worthy of higher accolades and accomplishments. I propose we launch **The Great Elevation,** where it is our duty to uplift and celebrate other people. We all need to support, encourage, love, celebrate, and champion each other because that is **HIGH VIBRATIONAL ENERGY**. When we vibrate from **HIGH VIBRATIONAL FREQUENCIES,** we can all achieve massive success and happiness collectively. We are all ONE. We were all created the same, and we are **ALL DESTINED FOR GREATNESS.** However, due to social programming and **The Great Suppression** of society, it has done a great job of clipping your wings and instilling **perpetual unworthiness** inside of you. **_Allow me to pluck the perpetual unworthiness out of you, so that you can permanently become a worthy human being._**

Being Offended

Being offended means someone else is allowed to have a perspective that is different from your own. I am a person who is **NEVER OFFENDED,** even by offensive things. **_I choose not to be offended._** I let things go in one ear and out the other. **_I choose not to be reactionary, ever._** People are allowed to think differently from you. They are allowed to have different thoughts, beliefs, and values. You should always respect other people's thoughts, beliefs, and values. It is important to always listen to someone else's perspective hearing their side of the story nonjudgmentally. People believe what they believe for a reason, whether it was programmed into their mind, or they concluded on their own through their intuition. **_When you understand and appreciate people for who they are and the value they bring to the table, you will no longer be offended by anything or anyone ever again._** Understanding and being offended cannot happen at the same time.

HARD

This section concerns the recognition and appreciation of how HARD life is. I am convinced that life is HARD for everyone, no matter your environment, situation, or circumstances. I do, however, believe that **WITH MONEY,** life is less HARD, so we will discuss money in another section of this book. If you are anything like me, life was never easy for you. *I cannot remember one time when my life was easy.* I have struggled in a myriad of ways my whole life; in fact, my middle name could arguably be Obstacle. I have faced obstacles at every turn in my life. I wish my life had been easier. I wish I didn't have to struggle, but I do believe that struggle is necessary and that it builds character. Without struggle, I would be just another entitled princess who thinks the world owes her everything. But it doesn't. *The world doesn't owe anybody anything.*

With that said, one of the best ways to combat **HARD** is to **PULL THE BULL BY THE HORNS.** What I mean is **TAKE ACTION / TAKE INITIATIVE**. You have the power to impact and change your environment, situation, and circumstances so that your life can become less **HARD. *Mitigating HARD will always prove to be advantageous for you.*** In addition to **HARD,** we also have **HEAVINESS. HEAVINESS** makes **HARD,** HARDER because it adds extra layers of stress and strain to the current obstacles you experience. *Heaviness* is when things just keep piling on top of one another, and before you know it, you feel like you are carrying around a ton of rocks on your back; it literally feels like you are carrying a cross.

We are not meant to do life alone, but many of us (especially as women) do not have a choice. I put emphasis on gender here specifically, because historically speaking, men have always had way more help/support compared to women both inside and outside of the workforce. If you are biblically versed, the Bible calls woman a Helpmate to man, and if you read my first book, **GIRL GRIT: SAVAGE NOT AVERAGE,** you will know by now how much I despise the word Helpmate. *Helpmate is one of the most cringeworthy words in the world because it suggests that men are allowed help, but women are not, yet it is women who need the help, because often, we are doing everything anyway.*

MY HEAVINESS and **MY HARD** come from being a parent. Your **HEAVINESS** and your **HARD** might also come from being a parent, or it could come from something or someone else, or a combination thereof. I love my daughter, and I would do anything for her, but being a parent does not come naturally to me. What comes naturally is being a businesswoman. Therefore, I struggle way more with parenting than I do with business. I do not find parenthood fun or rewarding; I find it to be work. By admitting this truth, I become more real to my readers, because **authenticity** matters in a fake world. This does not mean I don't love my daughter or that I am not engaged with her – it just means I must work extra hard to engage, be present, be focused on her, her needs, and her emotional wellbeing, which parents of earlier generations seemed to have ignored our emotional needs altogether to a greater or lesser degree. ***Back in those good old days, it was shameful to discuss your HARD. In fact, you were probably institutionalized for it, but today, I believe in authenticity and openness and that there is no shame in admitting your HARD or that you aren't perfect in every way as a woman.***

Our society places too many expectations on women and then wonders why we have mental breakdowns. Men seem to get away with things women would easily be blamed for even in today's world. ***This is an additional heaviness I feel, the heaviness due to gender and no other reason at all.*** Can we just acknowledge, accept, and appreciate that life is **HARD and HEAVY?**

HEAVINESS comes from **PRESSURE, EXPECTATIONS,** and **OBLIGATIONS.** Or what I call **THE THREE EVILS – 1) PRESSURE, EXPECTATIONS, and OBLIGATIONS.** Let's break this down further.

1. **PRESSURE** – The world is full of pressure, most of which is social. This pressure most often comes from others, or it could also come from within yourself. Pressure FEELS

HEAVY. Like rocks on your back. *Pressure is simply the HEAVY you feel.*

2. **EXPECTATIONS** – Expectations mostly come from others and sometimes yourself. It is a standard you are held to and accountable for.

3. **OBLIGATIONS** – Obligations are things you don't want to do. In fact, you don't want to do them or even enjoy doing them. You do them simply because you feel pressure and obligation to do them. *You FEEL like you OWE someone something.* That you are responsible for something you may or may not actually be responsible for – *it can be real or imaginary.*

What to do – *most things do not matter at all.* What this means is **EVALUATION** and **ANALYSIS.** If you feel pressure, expectations, and obligations, you need to evaluate and analyze their importance to you and your life. *People often FOCUS on things that do not matter much at all.* Those things add pressure and obligation to your life that do not need to be there. Most of your time and money are wasted on things that don't bring much value to your life. *An honest evaluation of these things will help you realize their impact and the possible damage they have caused you.*

For example.

When I was 23 years old, I worked at a Marketing Company that paid me $12/hr. because at the time, even with a college degree, I didn't know what I was worth. I accepted anything (which is another issue all on its own). Adding insult to injury, I spent two hours per day, five days per week, commuting since the company was an hour away from my home. Add insult to injury again, I lived in Cleveland, OH, and drove a small sedan. That winter, our weather was brutal, and the roads were awful. I spun out driving to work 5-7 times that winter on my way to or home from work, the scariest experience of my life. I am so lucky to be alive right now. *All for $12/hr.* Literally putting my life on the line every day for $12/hr. Because I thought I wouldn't eat or be able to pay my bills without that measly $12/hr. *I was majoring in minor things.*

Eventually, I did quit the job, but not because of the winter and bad roads, because I suffered massive burnout. I was forced to work weekends without extra pay. I was the hardest working person in the office, they **REWARDED** me with **MORE WORK, MORE RESPONSIBILITY, and NO increase in pay.** I worked 60-70 hours per week, making roughly $1600 per month after taxes while putting my life on the line every day, so yes, it took all of that to get me to eventually quit. That is how hardworking I was. Any employer would hire me after knowing that.

My dad, who worked 55 years of his life never calling off even when he was sick and immobile, told me verbatim, *"Yeah, you need to quit that job."* My dad never encouraged anyone to quit, but this situation was a ***horse of a different color.***

I was majoring in minor things. I was putting all this very **unnecessary pressure, expectation, and obligation** on myself to the point of not sleeping or eating. I went an entire week without sleep, and I lost 20 lbs. in a month. I couldn't sleep because I couldn't stop seeing the f*cking spreadsheet in my mind. *This job didn't matter at all.* I was prospering a company who didn't give a rat's ass about my mental health or wellbeing. They let me suffer. *They rewarded me with more work for hard work, and they inevitably lost an amazing employee because of their own greed and stupidity.*

Know Your Worth

Complete an ***honest evaluation of yourself*** concerning employment and what you are worth per hour. ***Your evaluation should include the following considerations.***

1. *Dollar amounts you are worth per hour.*
2. *Years of employment experience.*
3. *Education level.*

4. *Years at different companies (job longevity).*
5. *Certifications, courses, and additional credentials.*
6. *General knowledge and expertise.*
7. *Awards, associations, additional projects, and achievements.*

Let me give you another example. Three years ago, I was approached for a coaching job that offered $133/hr. Now, to the average person, this seems like a lot of money, right? Not to me. At that time, I was worth $700/hr., nearly **six times the amount offered.** I told the hiring manager this fact and told her (out of the kindness of my heart) I would work the job for no less than $350/hr. (cutting them a deal). She refused my counteroffer because they could only afford $133/hr. Okay, fine.

Two days later, she emails me and says, **"I want to be you someday."**

Today, I am worth $1,000/hr. for **Executive Coaching.** Soon, I will be worth $2,000/hr. and it will continue to go up from there.

The same is true for you.

The year is 2025. If you have 10 years of employment experience, a bachelor's degree, and a good skillset with decent credentials but are only making $50K/year, then you are grossly underpaid in my professional opinion. Yes, certain companies cannot afford to pay you any more than what you are currently being paid. However, **perspective is key.** You can easily leave the current employer and make $20-50K more per year to start. What a raise! The best way to make more money is to leave the current employer and get a new job.

I have come a long way from $12/hr. to $1000/hr. The year I made $12/hr. was 2013; today it is 2025. **ASCENSION IS THE ANSWER; remember that.**

Ascension is the Answer

In life, you will experience much suffering and many tragedies of various kinds. No one is immune to drama, trauma, catastrophe, or tragedies of all kinds. **The trick is how you deal, heal, and move on.** The answer to all pain and suffering, no matter how awful it is, *is ascension.*

Think of it this way – suffering is descension because you are in a **descended state of mind** when you are suffering, right? **The opposite of descension is ascension.** This is why ascension is the answer. **You can ascend in a myriad of ways.** Ascension isn't only about money and financial prosperity. **Ascension is about prosperity, and there are millions of ways to prosper.**

Different types of Ascension –

Emotional Ascension – rising of emotions, experiencing positive, feel-good, or heaven-state emotions.

Mental Ascension – mental sharpening and focus. Brightness and harmony of mind, body, and spirit connectivity.

Knowledge Ascension – brain power. Acquisition of new knowledge and skills will directly lead to making more money.

Financial Ascension – the act of making more money and building income-driven prosperity.

Health and Wellness Ascension – improvement of physical and psychological health and well-being.

Romantic and Sexual Ascension – the ability to have amazing sexual experiences that meet your specific sexual needs, coupled with romance, passion, desire, and erotic love.

Relationship and Marriage Ascension – the capacity to have healthy, life-giving, green flag relationships with partners, spouses, children, parents, friends, colleagues, acquaintances, business associates, clients, and the larger community.

Motivation Ascension – the ability to become more motivated, inspired, and productive. Making you more efficient and helping you conquer all goals and dreams.

The Ascension Connection

The best part about ascension is when you ascend in just one single area of your life, you magically and magnetically ascend in all others. This is part of the Law of Attraction. Success and all things are interconnected and compounded. You are creating a compounding effect for abundance and prosperity. ***For example, one of my own first ascension areas was Knowledge Ascension because at the time, I had nothing else going for me, but I got my ass in school and became a knowledge acquisition master. Through my education, I ascended in all other areas of my life a thousand-fold.*** DECIDE to ascend in just one area. Pick the area that is easiest for you so that it doesn't seem too overwhelming. ***For me, I just keep attracting more and more.*** Success begets success. ***Blessings fall out of the sky for me. I am the Universe's Golden Child; The Universe pisses glory on me. This can be you too!*** I won 21 awards in under 2 years, and I didn't even apply for most of them; I was literally sought after for them. ***I magically attracted those awards by continuing to ascend in all ascension areas.***

According to your FAITH it is done unto you. All things happen in DUE COURSE.

The Caveat

There is a caveat here, ***so mindfulness is key.*** Other people. Yes, other people are caveats. People who CHOOSE for whatever reason not to ascend hate ascenders because of their own self-sabotage and Fixed Mindset thinking. ***<u>Ascension is available for everyone. EVERYONE. LITERALLY.</u>*** I was not born rich, educated, or even happy. I come from humble blue-collar beginnings. ***I had nothing handed to me, not even help.*** Believe me when I say that **ASCENSION IS AVAILABLE TO EVERYONE,** no matter how you came into this world. Most of us came here with nothing.

Much of the world is poor or barely making ends meet. Even the middle class is struggling financially. Again, you **choose ascension. Be careful of non-ascenders.** I call non-ascenders **The Average** or the **Descending. The Descending** are actively throwing their lives away (criminals, addicts, alcoholics, haters, narcissists, jerks, assholes, **helpless people**) – they don't typically care about anything or anyone including themselves. **The Average** is 90% of society. They live life on autopilot without much excitement or adventure. **They are happy with mediocrity and the status quo. They are settlers.**

Be mindful and wary of these people. They will drag you down both consciously and unconsciously. You won't even know they are doing it because it is often subtle. For example, in my younger years, I was ascending magically in my career **(blessings falling out of the sky),** then I got romantically twisted with someone who systematically dismantled my self-esteem and everything going for me. **Aside from feeling jealous and inferior, this person chose not to ascend and decided that we cannot be on two different levels. This person decided to knock me off my Throne of Excellence, so that we could both be on his miserable level. It worked; I was knocked off. Next time someone tries to do that to me, I will march right out the door. My self-esteem is more important than my need for validation. Be careful of these people; they exist everywhere.**

The Village Within

As women, we could all use more help. No one wants to feel like they must do it all alone. Yet, many of us do. Many of us have no village. You either have a village or you don't, but we are told, it takes a village to raise a child. **I have come to learn that your village exists inside of you. The Universe is your SUGAR DADDY and HELPMATE.** The village is not an external reality. **It is an internal one, a guiding compass.** You have angels and archangels guiding and supporting you. They also offer help. You can think of your guardian angels and archangels as your helpers or village; they are always here to support and guide you on your journey through life. As a single mother myself, I have some help, but it is not enough; I am mostly on my own. I consider my guardian angels and my archangels my village. They are always there for me whenever I call upon them.

Christmastime as a Mother

I hope Christmastime brought fond memories for you as a child. I have fond memories of Christmas as a child. It was a time of rest and relaxation, two weeks off school, presents under the tree on Christmas morning, Breakfast with Santa, Christmas lights, Christmas concerts, decorating the tree, and a myriad of other happy memories. *It was a slow time of year.* However, Christmastime as a mother is a very different reality compared to childhood, and I often struggle to find joy in it at all.

I don't know about you, but as my year progresses, life gets busier and busier. For the most part, January-March for me is a huge come-down time since the craziness of the holidays is over. I live in Cleveland, OH, and the weather is usually nasty this time of year. There is no pressure to go outside. Mostly, I stay in and relax. April gets a little busier because of Easter and May is busier still because that is the last month of school. The school loves to pile a bunch of obligations and commitments for us mothers that last month.

My summers are not crazy busy, but because it is summertime, I am more active and involved in the summer compared to the winter months. Once school starts in September, my September and October get busier (far busier compared to summertime) because of school activities and commitments. The craziest busy times of year for me are no doubt November and December because of the holidays. The trend I notice, at least for me, is that as the months progress throughout the year, each month gets busier than the one before it. By

December, the end of the year, I am completely burnt out. It is no surprise I am writing this section in December 2024, and today is December 16th, 2024, precisely 9 days before Christmas Eve.

I must make a conscious effort to enjoy Christmas because, truthfully, as a mother, I do not enjoy it. For one, the family I created or thought I created got broken apart against my will so that shattered much of my zest for family, motherhood, and especially the holidays. *When I became a single mom, I became a sad single mom, because it wasn't the life "I signed up for," it wasn't the reason I walked down the aisle. My fate was handed to me on a silver platter, and I just had to accept it whether I wanted to or not.* I couldn't put myself up to getting Christmas photos with just my daughter and I as a single mom. I just couldn't do it. I lost far too much of my zest and happiness for holidays and family.

In addition to the sadness and loneliness of single motherhood, I soon discovered that Christmas was nothing but work FOR MOMS. No offense to the men of the world, but doesn't most, if not all, of the Christmas workloads fall on top of moms' shoulders? If mom doesn't put on the **Grand Christmas Show**, who else will do it? *So, yes, much of the work I do happens out of obligation to my daughter and owing her a mother who is not incessantly sad and angry that her life didn't exactly go as planned.*

I want to take a moment now acknowledging all the mothers right now who are doing this thing called Christmas. I don't know about you, but all I feel is pressure and heaviness. Perhaps there might be an ounce or two of joy to be squeezed out, but I assure you it is only an ounce or two of joy and nothing more. Even as I write these words right now, I feel like crying.

From shopping to wrapping to planning to cooking to hosting, the photos, the Christmas cards, the activities, the concerts, the school bullshit, the parties, the obligations, the commitments, how does it make any of you not scream at the top of your lungs? And then we have the audacity to work full-time outside of the home! Christmas makes me really f*cking sad. *I just wanted a real family, especially for my daughter.* Every kid deserves a real family. **_But the truth is, none of us can see the future._** If we could, we probably wouldn't have walked down the aisle that day. We probably wouldn't have gotten pregnant.

And the schools! Why? Why? It is the **universal dumping of commitments and obligations** this time of year, coming directly from my daughter's school, which runs my life. Can't the school give it a rest for heaven's sake? Every day, I pray and thank God I must only do this with one kid instead of two or three managing multiple teachers, homework, projects, friend groups, classrooms, and activities. I don't know how some of you keep it all together. Because I am about to lose my shit.

I try to give my daughter the best possible life you can imagine. I am a single mom. I do well for myself, but I am not rich. I work my ass off for everything I have. Nothing was ever handed to me. I have so little help, most of which I pay for. We live in a nice 4-bedroom house in a safe neighborhood. She goes to a private school, and she gets to go places and do activities all on my salary.

My boyfriend tells me I have the patience of a saint. I am an extremely emotionally grounded human being. That has taken mastery. I never ever yell at my kid, and I am proud as hell about that. The reason I don't yell is because the opposite of not yelling (which is yelling) is childhood abuse, and it does traumatize children to a greater or lesser degree. I write a lot about child abuse; I am very much against it and am an advocate for children. **All unhealed adults are capable of abusing their children.** Kids are exponentially stressful and frustrating, and my child is no exception. Even good kids are difficult. ***Parenting is just really f*cking hard and we do not*** *acknowledge the reality of it enough.* We really don't. *It takes every ounce of strength in my body not to yell and scream at my daughter when she doesn't listen or is whining.* I have mastered **emotional control and resilience**, but it has taken me years of healing, and I spend a great amount of time in meditation daily. Add all this bullshit to the bullshit of the Christmas stress and you can easily see why I want to run away right now.

"Oh, but they won't be little forever."

I want to punch people who say this. **You are completely invalidating my feelings.** Why don't we instead **admit and acknowledge** how hard parenting is, and instead say this to others experiencing difficulty in parenthood…

"I understand how hard being a parent is, it really is a challenge and a struggle. Some days, you want to run away or throw your arms up in the air and completely give up. Some days, you might not want to be a parent at all. I understand. It will be okay. This NOW moment will not last forever; no pain and suffering are forever. Everything will be okay."

In all seriousness, why does everything fall on mom? Just because of our gender? We must DO EVERYTHING. How about we start acknowledging our humanity and stop pretending and trying to be so perfect? I am so sick and tired of the act and the show. I miss when Christmas was slow. **I miss when Christmas was a time of rest and not work.** I miss when I got to open presents instead of having to wrap them for two weeks straight. I miss when Christmas was exciting and fun and not dreadful because it is busy, and you feel like you can't even get everything done in time because December flies by. I miss when life wasn't such a grind. **I miss being able to sleep at night without my mind racing a million miles an hour.**

Why all this pressure? What does it all mean? What would happen if we just quit? Not quit being moms but quit putting on **The Grand Christmas Show?** Stop doing backflips in the street naked for the school? ***Stop buying things people don't need.*** Stop all the stress and strain and just do nothing instead. ***Do nothing!*** We miss so much when we are rushing and racing around. ***I wish I had more answers for you, but the truth is, life is constantly changing, so nothing matters.*** Past Christmas stress doesn't matter. This Christmas stress doesn't matter. ***We can all learn how to slow down.***

No More Do Nothing at All – The Power of Slowness

We live in a world that moves ultra-fast. There is this invisible race to the finish line in everything as well as a race to the top. We race to fall in love, settle down, get married, have babies, get promoted, and retire. We chase and we race. Life is rush rush. Be here on time, pick up on time, and follow the routine and schedule. It all drives me crazy, this incessant busyness of life.

In this section, we will discuss the **Power of Slowness** and doing more by doing less. It is not necessary to busy yourself. There is only so much time in a day, a week, a month, and a year. Therefore, we must be selective with our time and energy, who we give it to, and how much of it we give. Pay attention to your time and energy identifying ways in which you are wasting time, whether small or significant. **Learn to slow down.** Stop doing so much. All you are doing is burning yourself out. This is no way to have a good quality of life. In *The Dynamic Laws of Prosperity*, Catherine Ponder asserts, "As you invoke the law of increase, remember that there is no hurry, force or push on the prosperous plane of life, and there is no lack of opportunity. Do all that you can do in a successful manner every day but do it as calmly as possible without undue haste, worry, or fear. Go as fast as you can, but do not hurry. The moment you begin to hurry, you cease to be prosperous in your thinking and become fearful, which is the prologue to failure."

I had a job where I worked the third shift, and some of my coworkers would sleep on the job because there was minimal work for us to do on the third shift. Our supervisor did not like this. One day, I came into the office to find a note for everyone on the third shift that read,

"No more, do nothing at all!"

It made me laugh because of the bad English, but the point is, she didn't want us doing nothing on the job.

My advice to you now is to **DO NOTHING AT ALL.** And that it is okay to **DO NOTHING AT ALL.** That doesn't mean become lazy and unproductive. I mean it is okay to take the necessary breaks and moments for yourself to literally **do nothing at all.** I go on two Zen trips per year (usually six months apart) where I spend five full days doing nothing at all except sleeping and meditating. That's right. I spend five full days, where all I do is sleep and meditate. I call it **doing nothing at all,** even though sleeping and meditating are real activities. **The point is I am completely away from all the noise and distractions of life.** I always take these trips alone and do my best to have the least number of conversations with people as possible for all five days. I am in complete rest and recharge mode. **Nothing can interfere with that time I have set aside for complete rest and recharge.**

Oftentimes, as women, we spend our time and energy doing things we don't want to do versus doing things we do want to do because we are always in some kind of caretaking role where other people depend on our time and energy. We give of ourselves without much being returned to us in a nurturing and caretaking capacity. Therefore, we must learn to care for ourselves as much as we care for everyone else around us.

One of the best ways to care for yourself is to **do nothing at all** implementing **The Power of Slowness.** For me, I hate rushing. I hate being late. I hate being in a hurry and feeling rushed, like I am on someone else's time and schedule. It is demanding and exhausting. It is okay to remove things from your plate so that you can make room for other things that truly matter.

Sister – Do nothing at all!

Chapter 11 Takeaways

- ➤ People play **Big Happy Family** maintaining impressions when the reality might be far more devastating.
- ➤ We glamorize and idolize pregnancy for no reason at all.
- ➤ We have lived most of our lives under **The Great Suppression.**
- ➤ Now is the time for **The Great Elevation.**
- ➤ Being offended means someone has a different perspective than you.
- ➤ Life is **HARD** and **HEAVY** – embrace it and don't push yourself beyond your emotional capacity.
- ➤ **Know your worth** because no one else does.
- ➤ Embrace **The Village Within** and stop putting on **The Grand Christmas Show.**
- ➤ **Learn the Power of Slowness and do nothing at all.**

Share Your Story:

In the space provided, it is time to share your story. How will you step into this time of **The Great Elevation**? How will you continue embodying your own human greatness? What can you remove from your plate? How will you practice the art of **do nothing at all?**

Chapter 12
The Celebrity Effect

The greatest definition of all time is I AM, for only we define ourselves – only we live our lives, therefore, we get to become exactly what we envision ourselves being."

"Once you make a decision, the universe conspires to make it happen." – Ralph Waldo Emerson

The Celebrity Effect

I want you to imagine right now that you are a celebrity. Ask yourself, do I want to be famous? Do I want to be a celebrity? Okay, I know not everyone reading this book wants to be famous. Some of you don't, I respect that. But even if you don't want fame, you can still embody what I call **The Celebrity Effect**. Another way to say this is **to fake it until you make it**. You've heard this because it is 100% true! You must start **WITH THE END IN MIND (Hathing)**. Act like and **pretend (hath)** that you **have** exactly what it is you want right now. **Open the palms of your hands now receiving whatever it is.**

I used to do this thing in seventh grade where I would **sign my homework** with my autograph, and it would piss off my teacher. At the top of the paper, where you should print your name, instead of printing my name, **I would sign my name AS IF I were signing an autograph.** I was signing the homework **AS IF. AS IF** I was already famous. The teacher would get upset, and she would always say repeatedly, *"Save that for when you're famous, Alex!"* **Two interesting things happened here: 1) I was acting AS IF. AS IF I was already who I wanted to be (hathing), and 2) she was speaking my future fame into existence.**

Do I want to be famous? Yes! Not for reasons of vanity, but rather for reasons of **IMPACT** and **INFLUENCE**. For reasons of **POWER.** The good kind of **POWER.** Leverage that power being a *force for good. With fame and fortune, I can help more people, and that is the name of the game, right?* To be of blessing and service to others. It is a lot harder to bless and serve others when you are poor than when you have the proper resources to do so. *How can you help someone else when you must first help yourself?*

Act like a Queen and you will be treated like one. I act like a Queen every day, and everyone around me treats me like one naturally. *People treat you the way you treat yourself.* This is *The Celebrity Effect* in motion. You absolutely must fake it until you make it. *First, no one will know the difference, and second, your subconscious mind doesn't know the difference between reality and imagination.*

Imagination comes first.
Then *Feeling* second.
Then the *manifestation* of your desires third.

In this order:

1. Imagination
2. Feeling (embodiment) + Faith
3. Manifestation – *from the unseen to the seen.*

I've used *The Celebrity Effect* in my business too because people are *more likely* to buy from someone who has amassed *some level of fame and recognition*. I've used it on my social media growing my social media audiences (buying followers, likes, comments, and views) because let's face it, your post is *more attractive/credible* when it has 1,000 likes and 30 comments compared to only 3 likes and no comments, right? That is *The Celebrity Effect.* All *influencers* buy followers, likes, comments, and views. Also, publicity matters. *Focus on building momentum and building your personal brand. You can do that by hiring a Publicist to help get your name and image out there.* Public relations are about *creating a story* around your brand. It is the *Celebrity Positioning* you need in the marketplace. *Why do you deserve to be in the spotlight? What legacy are you leaving behind in this world?*

Invest in Yourself

The best investment you will make is the investment in yourself. No one will ever invest in you the way you can invest in yourself. There is a myriad of ways to invest in yourself. Here are some examples:

- ➢ Putting yourself first and *being selfish (being selfish makes you selfless).*
- ➢ Fill your own cup FIRST.
- ➢ Get plenty of exercise and physical activity.
- ➢ Nurture your mind, body, and spirit.
- ➢ Invest in yourself financially.
- ➢ Buy yourself nice things – things you want and enjoy.
- ➢ Spoil yourself.
- ➢ Invest in programs, activities, courses, classes, and doing anything you love to do.
- ➢ Expand your mind – always learn, read, and become more educated.
- ➢ Grow your vocabulary with GRE vocabulary cards (available on Amazon).
- ➢ Limit time on social media and the phone. Go outside, meditate, and spend time in nature. *Nature has a profound healing element in it and can heal horrific trauma.*
- ➢ Spend lots of time alone, praying, meditating, and manifesting.

INVEST IN YOURSELF – INVEST IN YOURSELF – INVEST IN YOURSELF

Don't be stingy with money and do not hang on too tightly to it. If you are penurious with money, money will not flow effortlessly to you. *You must GIVE before you can RECEIVE.* Like they say, *"you have to spend money to make money."* Invest in yourself!

Here is a money affirmation for you today - *I invest lavishly in myself, and money always flows to me.*

Gratitude

Consistently step up your gratitude game. You must GO HARD with gratitude. Be thankful for all things you have and all things you do not have (hathing). ***Be thankful for your pain, suffering, and trauma, for without it, ascension and transformation are impossible.*** Be thankful for the big and small things.

Be thankful for:

> ➢ Your Life
> ➢ Body
> ➢ Mind
> ➢ 5 Senses
> ➢ Physical and Emotional Strength
> ➢ Family, Friends, Haters, and Enemies
> ➢ Clients and Employers
> ➢ The Ability to Learn and Ascend
> ➢ Your Children and Spouse
> ➢ Hard Times and Good Times
> ➢ Poverty and Wealth
> ➢ Fresh Air
> ➢ Nature
> ➢ The Roof Over Your Head
> ➢ Every Opportunity and Blessing
> ➢ Happy Memories
> ➢ Etc.

Make a list of 100-200 things to be thankful for. State your gratitude out loud every morning and every evening. ***Feel thankful every second of the day. Gratitude makes your life better. Gratitude eradicates all bad moods and negative feelings.***

Kids Laughing at Me

I remember being nine years old and wanting to make the world a better place. I used to tell other kids my age that someday I would help change the world, and their response.... they would laugh at me, and I didn't understand why. **Because I was dead serious.** I truly, deeply, and absolutely believed that I would help change the world someday. And remember, the subconscious mind cannot take a joke. **It believes everything you tell it. Because I absolutely believed in those words I said and felt, it became manifest.** I am helping to change the world today. I write books helping people transform and ascend. I am a Transformation and Empowerment Coach serving clients from all over the world. I have won 21 awards to date for my work. My clients tell me all the time that I am changing and saving lives, and my legacy is still only beginning as I am only 35 years old. **So much life ahead of me and plenty more work to be done.**

They laughed at me because they thought it was ridiculous. They didn't believe. **They don't understand just how powerful we all are.** This is my favorite quote of all time from Marianne Williamson:

"Our deepest fear is not that we are inadequate. Our deepest fear is that we are powerful beyond measure. It is our light, not our darkness, that most frightens us. We ask ourselves, Who am I to be brilliant, gorgeous, talented, fabulous? Who are you not to be? You are a child of God. Your playing small does not serve the world. There is nothing enlightened about shrinking so that other people won't feel insecure around you. We are all meant to shine, as children do. We were born to manifest the glory of God within us. It's not just in some of us; it's in everyone. And as we let our own light shine, we unconsciously give other people permission to do the same. As we are liberated from our own fear, our presence automatically liberates others."

Your need for greatness and excellence has got to be more important than your need to be liked and accepted by others.

When you play small, when you play it safe, you LAUGH in the Creator's face.

God does not make mistakes. Your insecurities sabotage you subconsciously.

It took me 34 years to understand and accept the fact that I am a lovable and worthy human being. 34 years! It was Tony Robbins who made me realize that as I was bawling my eyes out all alone in an auditorium filled with 14,000 people in Dallas, TX, in November 2023, at his event *Unleash the Power Within.* 34 years! And I am telling you that when I fully and completely **ACCEPTED WHOLEHEARTEDLY** that I am a **WORTHY** and **LOVABLE HUMAN BEING** my entire life **TRANSFORMED** within a second! A second! *34 years of pain, suffering, trauma, drama, and struggling all washed away just like that.*

I don't care what you've done.

I don't care what was done to you.

I don't care what kind of horrific trauma you've been put through.

I don't care what your biggest darkest secret is…

I want you to know without a doubt that you are a WORTHY and LOVABLE human being.

When I accepted that…. truly accepted it….

I was never rejected again. I was never hurt again. I have so much love rushing toward me right now, I cannot even manage it all!!!

ASCEND BABY – ASCEND!

Stop reading right now and stand up. Back completely straight. Tears rolling down your face, and open up your palms to the heavens. RECEIVE IT. RECEIVE IT. RECEIVE IT. AND RELEASE THE PAIN. RELEASE THE PAIN. RELEASE THE PAIN. TRANSCEND THE TRAUMA. TRANSCEND THE TRAUMA. TRANSCEND THE TRAUMA.

Say it over and repeatedly.

I AM A WORTHY HUMAN BEING.

I AM LOVABLE.

RECEIVE IT. RECEIVE IT. RECEIVE IT.

And so, it is… you are now healed.

The Pattern of Poverty and Wealth

Poverty and wealth are more conditions of the mind than they are realities. You can think wealthy, or you can think poorly. Most of us were conditioned to think poorly, which is why most people are poor and struggle to earn money. Poverty, like anything else, is passed down from generation to generation, which is why if your parents struggled, you will likely struggle too, but if your parents are wealthy, you are more likely to be wealthy. Poverty-thinking is a curse that must be dismantled at once. **You do not deserve to be poor; you deserve to be rich and wealthy. Wealth is a gift from God. God has created you for wealth, so that you will use that wealth to do God's will.** It is super hard to do God's will when you are broke. **Because when you are broke, you are working hard to earn money just to survive and live. You are so busy working that you have no time to do God's work. See how that works?** <u>**God wants you wealthy so you can serve and give back more.**</u>

This is why it is said that the poor become poorer, and the rich become richer. Law of Attraction at work again, like attracts like, you attract what you inherently are. Even though I was born into a middle-class family, I was not poor. *I cultivated a rich mindset even as a child, and my subconscious mind did what it does best; it led me to activities and opportunities where I could attract and create wealth for myself.*

You either get into a pattern of poverty or a pattern of wealth, and most of the middle class fall into the pattern of poverty. You must think wealthy and think of wealth before you become wealthy. ***Wealth and poverty are only defined in terms of the person embodying the experience of wealth or poverty.*** I consider poverty a reality where someone is struggling to make enough money to get by. If you are living paycheck to paycheck, in my mind, you are poor because there is no abundance. If you have enough money to save and go on vacation or afford other luxuries for yourself, then by definition, you are not poor; you are living abundantly. In *At Your Command* by Neville Goddard, he explains, "Life does not care whether you call yourself rich or poor; strong or weak. It will eternally reward you with that which you claim as true of yourself." He also expresses that, "It is impossible for the poor man to find wealth in this world, no matter how he is surrounded by it, until he first claims himself to be wealthy. For signs follow, they do not precede. To constantly kick and complain against the limitations of poverty while remaining poor in consciousness is to play the fool's game."

The Wealthiest Girl Alive

I consider myself to be the wealthiest girl alive, not because I was born into a wealthy family, but because of the brain in my head and the heart in my chest. I was born into an average American middle-class blue-collar family. I would consider us to be middle class or lower-middle class, because even though we were always provided for, money was tight and travel non-existent. I think many of you can resonate with this type of family because America was built by the working middle class. I was thoroughly provided for, and my physical needs were met, but we did not live large, travel, or even wear name-brand clothes ever. I did not know name brands until my late 20s. *For my childhood, I am extremely thankful. My childhood taught me to take pride in hard work, not to make excuses, that there is no shame in hard work. It also taught me to be humble and appreciate everything in life, no matter how big or small. As all parents do, my folks did the best they could for us with all the resources provided to them, and so for that, I am extremely wealthy.*

Had I been born into financial wealth, my life would have been far easier, and I wouldn't have had to work, and maybe that luxurious lifestyle would have been nice. I do not know because I have never experienced that reality. But something happened, something I cannot put my finger on, honestly. My mom will tell you that I spent considerable time as young as two years old meditating and reflecting deeply on everything and anything. That very practice is called **VISUALIZATION**, which is the essence of manifestation because your brain doesn't know the difference between **REALITY** versus **IMAGINATION**. Pretty cool, huh? **When you meditate or visualize, you GROW your brain.** It is called **Neuroplasticity,** or the growth/expansion of brain capacity. That is what happened; my imagination ran wild, and my brain power grew exponentially.

This is why I am the **wealthiest girl alive**; it is because of the brain I have been given. I have said this before, and you will hear me say it a million more times, your brain is the most **POWERFUL ASSET** you own. You have heard it said that most people only use 10-20% of their brain, and I can understand why. **They do not bother to grow their brains.** They have a Fixed Mindset versus a Growth Mindset (I have a **Growth Mindset** and so do you). <u>***It is not money that makes you wealthy, it is your human mind.***</u>

I couldn't read until I was 11 years old, yet I am the most successful person in my immediate circles. How can it be so? The mind can do miraculous things. Your mind is your **powerhouse.**

It is where all your power comes from. *Focus on things that GROW your mind.*

For example – remove yourself from the following distractions that reduce brain power:

- ➤ Watching the negative news
- ➤ Talking to negative people
- ➤ Gossip and hate talk
- ➤ Email and text notifications
- ➤ Social Media
- ➤ TV
- ➤ Hanging out with non-ascender friends
- ➤ Giving to others who never give back to you
- ➤ Self-sacrifice
- ➤ Fast food, processed food, and sugar
- ➤ Alcohol or drugs

Do these things which increase brain power:

- ➤ Read, read, read! READ!
- ➤ Go back to school
- ➤ Get certifications and or take courses
- ➤ Listen to educational podcasts
- ➤ Exercise
- ➤ Eat Healthy
- ➤ Drink Water
- ➤ Get plenty of Sleep
- ➤ Nature Walks
- ➤ Listen to Smoothing Music
- ➤ Massages
- ➤ Meditation and Relaxation
- ➤ Brain Puzzles or Games
- ➤ Minimal Screen and TV Time
- ➤ Reduce Social Media
- ➤ Create Plans and Execute on Them
- ➤ Hang out with Motivated and Successful People
- ➤ Remove all Negativity and Toxicity

> *Stop Being a People-Pleaser and Glutton for Punishment – BIG ONE!!!*
> Stop doing menial tasks that do not advance you in life

I did not grow up with material wealth. There were things I wanted and never got. But there is one thing that has made me massively successful, and that is **STRUGGLE**. Struggle is extremely motivating and empowering. *People who do not struggle have no reason to ascend.* The most successful people in this world are those who struggled and suffered the most. *For my struggles and suffering, I am extremely thankful. For the mind I was given, I am extremely thankful, for my mind has taken me places that money never could. My mind has made all my dreams come true, and it has manifested my every wish and desire to complete and total fulfillment. And for that, I am the wealthiest girl alive. Because no amount of money can replace a God-given beautiful mind.* Only God can create something as powerful as your mind. Do not waste your mental capacities. *Appreciate them every day, and you will be given everything your heart desires and then some.*

Asking

The reason why people do not get what they want is because they do not ask for it. Most people are **ASK-SHY.** They hate asking for things because they feel bad and greedy about it. The Bible clearly says, *ask and you shall receive.* That verse is so clear that you cannot miss the meaning. I used to be **ASK-SHY,** because I have always been more of a giver than a taker. *I had to learn how to RECEIVE, because I only knew how to GIVE.* Learn to **RECEIVE.** I read an entire book about asking called *The Aladdin Factor* by Jack Canfield, and that book taught me how to ask for the things I want in any aspect of life. **ANY ASPECT – work, school, friends, family, social, hobbies, finances, health, etc.** In *The Aladdin Factor* by Jack Canfield, he states, "Most of us don't know how to ask. We have never learned the technology of making an effective request. We have not seen these effective communication skills modeled in our homes, and we were not taught them in our schools or at work. Many of us don't know whom to ask and when to ask."

Women are raised to be nurturers and caregivers (we ARE NOT naturally nurturing or caregiving, that, like anything else, is a **_learned behavior_**). We are conditioned to become **givers** because that becomes our role in society. **We become givers, so everyone around us can become takers. Some women have not yet realized that selfishness makes you selfless.** Because we were programmed to become givers, we have NO IDEA how to ASK for anything. **We often feel like we do not have the right to ask because we are perceived as givers because of our gender and no other criteria.**

Learn how to become a TAKER. **Learn to RECEIVE. Learn to ASK.** Force yourself out of your comfort zone. **All relationships depend on healthy giving and taking.** This is called **_reciprocity._** It is wrong to be just a giver, and it is equally wrong to be just a taker. **A full human being learns to give and take equally, promoting equality and well-being.**

Start asking for anything you want. Practice asking and ask as often as you want for anything you want. Notice how much more you receive. You don't have to do everything, and you don't have to be everybody's everything; you are not superwoman. Leave the dishes in the sink, let the laundry pile up, don't pick up after anybody, let the beds stay messy. **Doing menial tasks DO NOT PROSPER YOU AS A HUMAN BEING, and they certainly won't make your dreams come true.**

Different Types of Abundance

When people think of abundance, they often think of it in terms of wealth and money. **Abundance means a plentiful quantity of something.** In which areas of your life do you seek abundance or **plentiful quantity?** Abundance manifests in terms of:

> ➢ Health Abundance (mental, physical, and spiritual)

- ➢ Wealth Abundance (finances)
- ➢ Relationship Abundance (friends, partners, family, and network)
- ➢ Intelligence and Creativity Abundance (innate mental faculties)
- ➢ Emotional Abundance (feel-good emotions and happy memories)
- ➢ Material Abundance (possession of material goods that enrich life)
- ➢ Knowledge Abundance (acquisition of knowledge and the capacity to learn)
- ➢ Nature Abundance (the abundance of nature and natural beauty)

Can you think of other categories of Abundance to add here?

The Big Three: Wealth, Relationships, and Health

The three most prominent areas of anyone's life include ***Wealth, Relationships, and Health.*** Wealth is how we make a living sustaining ourselves here on earth. Without money, we can't buy anything, support ourselves, and stand on our own two feet as independent adults. Money is the lifeblood of our existence. It is something everyone seeks, earns, and always wants more of. Even people who have amassed serious wealth always seek to gain more.

Our lives are comprised of all kinds of relationships, including the families we are born into, the partners and significant others we choose, extended family, classmates, friends, colleagues, coworkers, church family, and other social circles and networks. Relationships encompass a central portion of our lives requiring a lot of our time, given the situation. Finally, our health is everything (physical and mental). Without good physical and mental health, we would not be able to earn money and may struggle sustaining healthy relationships.

It is important to equally nurture all three areas of your life. Complete an analysis of your life in each of these *three central areas.* Ask yourself, how am I performing in each area? Is any area lacking or suffering? *Make sure you are fulfilled and aligned in each area.* What needs to improve? What changes must you make in any given area? *It is important to be aligned, whole, and satisfied in all three areas, because each of these three areas gives plenty of abundance.*

Sister - You were born to sparkle and shine. You have **The CELEBRITY EFFECT.**

Chapter 12 Takeaways

> ➤ Fake it until you make it. ***This is called The Celebrity Effect.***
> ➤ Act *as if* you already have it (the art of hathing) and *be grateful that it is here now.*
> ➤ *Gratitude is the secret to having anything you want.*
> ➤ Wealth and Poverty are both *conditions of the mind* and not realities.
> ➤ Wealth does not come in the form of money or materials, *but rather in the form of your mind and human imagination.*
> ➤ Ask for anything you wish. *Master the art of asking.*

Share Your Story:

In the space provided, it is time to share your story. How will you use **The Celebrity Effect** to manifest all your dreams and desires?

Chapter 13
Snow Globe

"As I look into my Snow Globe, I relive every happy memory. I remember how good life has been for me. I only cherish and never complain, for cherishing produces more and complaining produces lack."

"Silence is the ultimate weapon of power" – Charles de Gaulle

Snow Globe

Time is like a Snow Globe. Our lives are filled with ***experiences, circumstances and lessons.*** Some positive and some negative, some wanted and some unwanted. In coaching, we teach our clients to always **LIVE IN THE PRESENT or LIVE IN THE NOW.** The past is done and over with, and the future is yet to be. ***All we have is THE NOW.*** This helps us remain focused and present in the moment. I often dream of the future because I am constantly creating and manifesting it for myself. ***But I do not live in the future.***

If you read my second book, ***GIRL GAME: BALLS OUT,*** you read the story about Electric Blue. ***I only spent a total of five, maybe six hours with this person, but that day was the best day of my life, and that experience meant the world to me.*** Earlier in this book, you read about how Electric Blue came back a year later and then ended up blocking me, well, the story is not quite over yet. ***He reached out again, a second time, three months after he had blocked me.*** After being blocked, I was sure I'd never hear from him again.

Here is what he had to say:

"I'd like to meet you again. I have never had the kind of connection with anyone that I've had with you. I know I have been

unreliable, but I'd like to give us another chance, if I don't, I may miss something special."

I replied 24 hours later, and this was my response:

"You're right. What we had last summer was special and rare, which is why I don't understand why you disappeared. I cared about you, and I was only trying to be your friend. I didn't ask for a commitment. I don't understand why you thought you could replace me. So many unanswered questions..."

After I responded (24 hours later), I discovered that I had been blocked... again!! For the second time!

It's obvious this boy is unhealthy, insecure, and dramatically fears rejection.

What we had that summer exists now only in a Snow Globe. That day didn't just mean something to me, it meant something special to both of us. I taught Asher just as much as he taught me. Although we were never meant to be together, we were destined to be in each other's' lives for a brief period like two ships passing in the night. Kismet. **I never lost Electric Blue. Electric Blue lost me.** I never scared him away. I never acted fast, needy, or insecure. I was always patient, gentle, thoughtful, and empathic toward him. He felt inadequate next to me, as if he had nothing to offer me.

But he was wrong.

He had everything to offer me.

He made me feel so seen, wanted, and desired.

<u>**What the f*ck is that worth?**</u>

Yes, maybe he was young and couldn't offer money, stability, commitment, time, or what have you, but that boy made me feel f*cking seen, wanted, and desired. What is that worth?

**It's worth everything.**

We all just want to be seen.

We all just want to be wanted.

We all just want to be desired.

We all just want to f*cking matter to someone.

It is our core emotional need.

Snow Globe.

A moment in time.

Dancing in the sand, around and around in circles, laughing, child-like, carefree, unbothered, happy, blissful, loved, seen, wanted, wanted, wanted, wanted, around and around and around in a Snow Globe, on the sand, by the water, summertime, laughter, smiles, happy, passion, excitement, ecstasy. **To be fully present, in the now, in the moment** – _the sweetest, happiest, best day of my life. Gifts._ **Moments are gifts. Electric Blue was a gift.**

He thought he gave me nothing, but he gave me everything.

He will grow older, he will get married, and he will have 2-3 children of his own with another woman. From time to time in his 30s, 40s, 50s, 60s, 70s, and even 80s he will look inside of his **Snow Globe,** and he will see me there _dancing on the sand by the beach_ with his arms around me. He will notice the happiest brightest smile on my face, and it will make him smile too. **And he will think fondly of me. A smile will stretch across his face every time the memory of me appears.**

Because as he walked out my door that night turning around to look at me one more time, the last time I ever saw him, I looked him in the eyes, and I said: **Absence makes the heart grow fonder.** _And as he walked out my door that night, eyes locked on me, not breaking the stare, he said,_ **"It does, it really does…"**

<u>*Our permanent absence will make him miss me forever. I will never age. I will never grow tired. I will always be perfect and happy, locked away in his Snow Globe, where I belong.*</u>

A Really Good Meal

Lou is my best friend; he knows everything about me, and we talk almost every day. I told Lou that Electric Blue had reached out again. This is what he had to say about the whole situation.

*"You know that situation, is like **A Really Good Meal.** You eat it and you enjoy it in the moment, the here and now, but it doesn't last forever. Once it's gone, it's gone, **and you should never think about it again."***

*Lou is right. My day with Electric Blue was like **A Really Good Heal,** one that I will savor locked away in my **Snow Globe.** When I close my eyes on my deathbed reflecting on all the hell life has put me through, I will look over at my **Snow Globe** and see myself on that beach dancing in the sand. I will close my eyes and smile knowing that I lived. I really f*cking lived.* <u>**Knowing that I am loved beyond comprehension. I'm really f*cking loved.**</u>

Nothing Matters

Nothing matters. The past doesn't matter, and neither does the future. All we have is the **present moment.** All you own is your **own consciousness,** fueled by your five senses, and that shapes your human experiences. **Nothing is real; therefore, it doesn't exist at all.** Yet, we spend most of our lives worrying about everything and everyone, much of which we have no control over anyway. **Some of us have too much responsibility, while others have too little. Some of us are burdened by our gender, while others are privileged by it. The same is true of our race.** We live our lives on timelines rushing and racing to every finish line imaginable – get a job, get married, have kids, get promoted, retire, and die.

Most of our lives are spent working. When we are children, we work on our chores and on our studies. In our adult lives, we must work to make a living and survive. We only get two days off per week on the weekend, *barely enough time to recharge.* *Too many of us are people-pleasers because we were raised to be perfect and to never disappoint others.* Our children (if they are privileged) appreciate nothing we do for them, taking most things for granted because they have not lived their lives in struggle and strife like less fortunate children have. *If our spouses cheat on us, that is because they have not learned how to be satisfied with what they do have. They are only amused by precisely what they don't have.*

Many of us do not eat well because we are stressed, and for the same reason, we also don't sleep well. *Our lives are filled with anxiety, nervousness, and uncertainty instead of profound joy and peace. Everyone takes advantage of us because we haven't learned our own worth yet.*

What does it all mean? Frankly, it doesn't mean anything. *It means you are focused and fixated on things that do not matter at all.* Look at your life as if it were a book with each phase representing a chapter. *Does anything from your past matter today?* Does today matter today? Do you catastrophize often? Do you make things a much larger issue than what they actually are? Do you allow people, situations, and circumstances to stress you out? *Are you constantly worried about the unknown or what might happen next?*

Nothing matters. You live, and someday you will die. ***All you own is your own consciousness and awareness of your human existence.***

Has life been fair to you? Probably not.

You have probably suffered more than you'd like to admit.

Your heart has probably been broken more than it has been mended.

You might have been screamed at more as a child than you were hugged or perhaps loved at all.

You might have many regrets – mostly good intentions that went astray.

You've probably been stepped on more times than you've felt powerful.

Rejection might be your middle name by now. That or Unworthy.

So, what does it really all mean?

Were you put here to suffer?

Were you put here to be raped?

Were you put here to be screamed at?

Were you put here to be physically and emotionally assaulted?

Were you put here to be the outcast or the scapegoat?

Were you put here to be bullied?

Were you put here to be riddled with anxiety and Depression?

Were you raised to be perfect and not a human being?

Were you raised to be a gender and not a human being?

Have you been discriminated against because of your gender, age, or skin color?

Have you been hated because of your gender, age, or skin color?

Were you put here to be gossiped about?

Were you put here to work a job you hate?

Were you put here to be a single mom and "do it all alone?"

Were you put here to be rejected and discarded or cheated on?

Were you put here to financially struggle all your days?

Were you put here to be grossly underpaid for your labor?

Silver Lining

In all situations, no matter how bad they seem, there is always a silver lining. ***ASCENSION cannot happen without remarkable pain and suffering. Pain and suffering are the catalysts launching you into unimaginable greatness.*** My life was hallmarked by pain and suffering in a myriad of ways. My teenage years were spent thinking about suicide.

I was 16 years old and Googling ***painless ways to kill yourself.*** I couldn't withstand the unfair storms of life. The pain, rejection, loneliness, unworthiness, Depression, anxiety, and isolation I felt throughout my life. I thought the solution was to end the pain and suffering for good. It took me several years to learn that the only thing one can do with their pain is to transcend it and ASCEND. ***My pain made me the resilient force I am today. They say God won't give you anything you can't handle. That is another giant crock of shit. God doesn't give you anything. You give it to yourself. You are the great I AM, your own <u>God consciousness.</u> There WILL BE pain and suffering, and plenty of it. It's not about "handling" pain and suffering. <u>It's about transcending that pain and ASCENDING!</u>***

19 years ago....19 years ago, I had seven unsuccessful suicide attempts.

I lie there, 16 years old, tears flowing down my cheeks, lying in a hospital bed. ***I had only two choices...***

I could continue to lie there afflicted by trauma, or I could transcend it by making an impact on others going through the same suffering. I chose the latter, but it takes courage. **It takes COURAGE to CHOOSE to RISE ABOVE YOUR CIRCUMSTANCES.**

It takes courage to say, "I deserve better, and I will not settle anymore!"

Ascend, baby, ascend!

I am living proof that you do not need to be a victim of circumstances but can be a TITAN OF TRANSFORMATION.

Although our pain and suffering seem like the worst thing that has ever happened to us, it is the best thing that has ever happened to us.

When I decided to wake up each day and place my **Crown of Worthiness** upon my head, my whole life transformed overnight.

You are a TITAN OF TRANSFORMATION!

The Future

I want you to become the woman who turns heads consciously and subconsciously when she walks in the room by harnessing all these **innate powers** that live inside of you now. A powerful woman can disarm anyone. Project yourself 10, maybe 20 years into the future. **What kind of woman are you becoming?** *If you are not becoming, then you are remaining, and if you are remaining, you may be remaining in:*

- ✓ Unworthiness
- ✓ Rejection
- ✓ Hopelessness
- ✓ Powerlessness
- ✓ Fear
- ✓ Doubt
- ✓ Anxiety
- ✓ Depression
- ✓ Suppression
- ✓ Frustration
- ✓ Envy

At this time, swim in oceans of worthiness, gratitude, hopefulness, acceptance, love, empowerment, certainty, faith, and elevation. **Watch how everything you touch turns to gold.**

20 years ago, I couldn't see today. **_But I had total faith._** I projected myself into where I am right now, and where I am right now is not where I want to be forever, so yet again, I am projecting myself 20 more years into the future.

Practice this exercise when you are experiencing feel-bad emotions.

When you are feeling negative emotions, anchor in positive emotions. Think about what you want to have and who you want to become. Think profoundly about that **magical life** you envision for yourself. Think about the wealth you want to have, the career, the family, the home and location, the impact and influence, and the things you want to do or achieve – anchor them now. **Close your eyes and anchor them in. Experience them "as if" they are happening to you right now feeling those positive emotions.**

You want everything you want in life because of the emotions those things will give you, but you can experience those emotions now while not having the things you want because you can **anchor in the emotions.** Any time you feel bad, do this experiment keeping yourself vibrating at a high level. To manifest huge things, you must feel good all the time or as often as possible. **Use this anchoring technique. Manifestation is about visualization and experiencing what you want as if it were happening now, pretending you already have it. Act as if you have it now (hathing) expressing gratitude that you have it now. _It is making its way to you now._**

I do not come from a family of privilege or opportunity. How can it be so? How can I be this magnetic attractor who has made every one of her dreams a reality and then some? **Everything you will must come to pass.** Your mind is bringing you your every want, wish, and desire. **The only thing standing in your way between right now and what you want is _timing_. _Divine timing._** Everything that has happened to you has made you who you are today – the good, the bad, and the ugly. **Your pain has been** *strategically placed in your life helping you ascend. <u>Those without pain and suffering have no need for ascension.</u>*

What really matters if nothing matters at all?

The only thing that matters is **human ascension.**

You, born into the world as an individual, are here for a **DIVINE PURPOSE,** and that **DIVINE PURPOSE IS <u>HUMAN ASCENSION.</u>**

How you ascend does not matter – **all that matters is that you ascend.**

You will ascend when you take your innate qualities, strengths, abilities, talents, and skills and manifest them into **purpose and potential.**

For me, that is through writing, coaching, training, artistic expression, and entrepreneurship. Yours will look different than mine.

How to Become a Full Human Being

Many people are fake; they wear masks in society. Who they are in public is often different than who they are behind closed doors. Being fake or carrying a façade does not make you a full human being. This is the problem with **Impression Management**; it is just a projection onto the world that isn't real.

How to become a Full Human Being:

1. BE HONEST / REAL / AUTHENTIC
2. HAVE BIG DREAMS AND BIG GOALS
3. SET HEALTHY BOUNDARIES AND STICK TO THEM
4. TAKE CARE OF YOURSELF FIRST AND FOREMOST
5. COMMAND RESPECT FROM OTHERS
6. BE KIND, GENTLE, LOVING, AND UNDERSTANDING
7. SHOW EMPATHY
8. BE BRAVE AND RESILIENT

9. SMILE
10. EXPRESS GRATITUDE AS OFTEN AS POSSIBLE
11. LAUGH
12. EMBRACE ALL OF LIFE'S HIGHS AND LOWS
13. TAKE OWNERSHIP OF YOUR SELF-HEALING JOURNEY
14. CONSTANTLY DEVELOP YOUR TALENTS AND SKILLS
15. EVOLVE AND GROW
16. DO NOT SPREAD ANY HATE OR NEGATIVITY
17. DO NOT GOSSIP OR BELITTLE OTHERS
18. LEARN HOW TO GIVE AND RECEIVE
19. RECEIVE ABUNDANCE AND BLESSINGS
20. HAVE A POSITIVE IMPACT ON SOCIETY

Do something big for the world beyond yourself. Yes, take care of your family, but focus on your mission. Focus on your potential and purpose.

Death – Ultimate Ascension

This book series teaches you how to ascend, empowering you to ascend and become your **highest self.** Let's consider death. Most people are afraid to die. Death is understood as a negative thing, as it is the end of life as we know it. ***But death is good; it means you have served your purpose here in the physical world, and you are transcending into the next world or realm of existence.*** In our Christian nation and Christian worldview, many believe in heaven and hell as places one goes when one dies. The only validity we have concerning heaven and hell is found in scripture (The Bible). Eastern religions and cultures hold other beliefs; they do not believe in heaven and hell. Their realities and beliefs are considerably different than ours here in America from a Christian perspective. We are taught that our faith in Christ bestows us a seat in heaven, and our lack of faith in Christ renders us a seat in hell.

When I studied World Religions back in college, the literature told us that people go exactly where they believe they are going,

<u>which makes a lot of sense to me, because it is in alignment with their faith and personal beliefs.</u>

I do believe in God, and in my understanding of her, **I do not believe in hell.** I believe hell is a fear tactic scaring people and getting them to behave in certain ways, keeping society conditioned and humanity limited. ***Most of us already experience hell here on earth. How could it get any worse for some of us? If we no longer have a physical body, then how would it be physiologically possible to burn in hell? It wouldn't be.*** You can't be burned if you don't have a physical body; therefore, there is no fire in hell. ***In the concept of eternity, how can God allow someone to suffer eternally? If their end was eternal suffering and damnation, then why would God create that person in the first place just for them to end up suffering eternally in hell without reprieve?***

One of my Christian friends taught me that everything is fiction (yes, including the Bible). This is a powerful statement, ***everything is fiction.*** That would suggest that nothing is fact. In marketing / public relations, we are taught that ***everything is an illusion.*** This is all based on perception, just bear with me as I defend my case.

Yes, everything is based on human PERCEPTION. Which is why you can change your perception, your thoughts, your emotions, and your beliefs, as previously addressed earlier in this text. ***You can make a case for anything because it is all based on perception.***

Does this suggest that life and the afterlife are illusory? Yes, it does. All you have is your mind and body. That is your reality. You have literally created your own life, and all that is your life today is an accumulation of choices you have made over the past several years since you were born. Now the question becomes fact or fiction? Well, neither. ***Everything is subject to perception and interpretation. What you believe to be a fact will be a fact to you.*** What you believe to be fiction will be fiction to you. *What you believe is real is real, and what you believe is illusion is illusion. Your mind is in control of it all.*

This is why I do not believe in hell. As an Empowerment Coach, we are not in the business of damning people, we are in the business of empowering people. Therefore, sin is damnation. *We only build people up; we do not drag them down. We tell them they are good and worthy, and not bad and unworthy, because remember, the subconscious mind believes anything you tell it at face value.*

Have we all made mistakes? Yes. Are any of us perfect? No. But that doesn't make you unworthy. *I believe in redirecting choices.*

For example, if someone has a habit of stealing – we wouldn't damn that person making them feel like a criminal, we will redirect the behavior, provide more education, and an opportunity to transform the behavior of stealing. We would lift them up by empowering them through transformation instead of punishing and condemning them. *All unwarranted behavior is the result of unaddressed and severe trauma.*

Death is ultimate ascension. *Every time something bad happens to you, you are ascending HIGHER.* That means when things are stagnant or good, you are remaining on your current level, but when something unfortunate happens, such as a divorce, breakup, death, loss of a job, storm, etc., do not be afraid. That means it is time to level up and ascend. *It is a warning that you are not meant to remain stuck where you currently are.*

Death is simply leaving one life or realm of existence to enter the next, and the purposes you will serve there. *This is why pain and suffering are not a bad thing if you listen to what your pain and suffering are teaching you.*

Sister – You are a Titan of Transformation.

Chapter 13 Takeaways

> ➢ Store happy memories and positive experiences away in your **Snow Globe,** forever cherishing them and their blessing in your life.
> ➢ **Nothing lasts forever. Happy memories are like A Really Good Meal.**
> ➢ **Nothing matters at all –** we are only passengers in this life, transitioning from one realm of existence into the next.
> ➢ Find the lessons and silver lining in all situations.
> ➢ Continuous improvements mean always becoming a full human being.
> ➢ **Death is ultimate ascension,** passing from one reality to the next.

Share Your Story:

In the space provided, it is time to share your story. How will you become a **Titan of Transformation** empowering (instead of disempowering) all of those around you?

Dr. Alexandra Elinsky provides life, relationship, career, and executive coaching services for clients globally.

To coach with Dr. Alexandra Elinsky, you may get ahold of her via the contact methods below:

Office number – 440.812.1612

Email – team@empowerhp.org

Connect on LinkedIn – Alexandra Elinsky, PhD

Connect on Instagram – Alexandra Elinsky, PhD/bossdivalibra

Or use this link to schedule your discovery session https://calendly.com/teamempoweryou/60min

References

Byrne, Rhonda. *The Power*. İstanbul, Artemis Yayınları, 2011.

Canfield, Jack, and Mark Victor Hansen. *The Aladdin Factor*. New York, Berkley Books, 1995.

Chopra, Deepak. *The Spontaneous Fulfillment of Desire*. Crown Publishing Group, 2004.

Chopra, Deepak. *The Seven Spiritual Laws of Success: A Practical Guide to the Fulfillment of Your Dreams*. San Rafael, Calif., Amber-Allen Pub, 1994.

Esther And Jerry Hicks. (2011). *Ask and it is given*. Hay House UK Ltd.

Goddard, Neville. *At Your Command*. Gildan Media LLC aka G&D Media, 11 May 2020.

Greene, Robert. *The 48 Laws of Power*. London, Profile, 1998.

Greene, Robert. *The Concise Mastery*. London, Profile Books, 2014.

Greene, Robert. *The Laws of Human Nature*. Penguin Usa, 2018.

Hill, Napoleon, and W Clement Stone. *Success through a Positive Mental Attitude*. New York, Ishi Press, 2013.

Norman Vincent Peale. *The Power of Positive Thinking; And the Amazing Results of Positive Thinking*. New York, Fireside/Simon & Schuster, 2005.

Ponder, C, and Catherine Ponder. *The Dynamic Laws of Prosperity*. Prentice Hall, 1973.